The Enigmatic Eye

Cover design by Don Munson
Book design by Iris Bass
Author photograph by Stephen Fischer

The Enigmatic Eye

MOACYR SCLIAR

Translated by
Eloah F. Giacomelli

AVAILABLE
PRESS

BALLANTINE BOOKS • NEW YORK

An Available Press Book
Published by Ballantine Books

Translation copyright © 1989 by Eloah F. Giacomelli

All rights reserved under International and Pan-American Copyright
Conventions. Published in the United States of America by Ballantine
Books, a division of Random House, Inc., New York, and simultaneously
in Canada by Random House of Canada Limited, Toronto. Originally
published in Portuguese as *O Olho Enigmatico* by Editora Guanabara
S. A., Rio de Janiero in 1986.

Library of Congress Catalog Card Number: 88-92185

ISBN 0-345-35969-0

Manufactured in the United States of America

First American Edition: March 1989

Why is it that the dying don't shed tears?

Max Frisch—*Questionnaire*

CONTENTS

THE ENIGMATIC EYE

A MAN GOES TO A MUSEUM.

He is a wealthy man; in fact, one of the wealthiest men in the country. He is not an art enthusiast, neither does he have a special liking for museums; as a matter of fact, he is not in the habit of frequenting public places. And yet, there he is, piqued by the same curiosity that has drawn thousands of people every day to this small, and in all respects, uninteresting museum. He is there to see the small painting that a custodian found in the basement, buried under a pile of loose-joined frames—a painting which, after being examined by both national and foreign experts, was pronounced to be nothing less than an original by Rafael Sanzio. How it ended up in this museum is a mystery. Anyway, there it is, the masterpiece, exposed to the admiring eyes of the public. It is a portrait of an old man of aristocratic bearing. What impresses visitors the most is his gaze, which is truly enigmatic.

The portrait fascinates the man as nothing else in the world—

whether it be magnificent landscapes, or luxurious buildings, or precious jewelry—has ever fascinated him. In the half light of the air-conditioned room (the preservation of this piece of art requires special conditions), he spends countless hours; the guard has to warn him that the museum is about to close, and that he must leave now. He leaves; but on the following day there he is again, motionless, magnetized. Finally, he makes a decision: The painting must be his. In order to reach this objective, he is willing to spare no expense and to run all kinds of risks.

There is one person he can turn to for this purpose—Jorge: In addition to being an aide, he is also a devoted friend and a jack-of-all-trades. The man sends for Jorge and entrusts him with his wish. Leave it to me, says Jorge. And indeed, three days later, Jorge hands a cardboard box over to the man. With trembling hands he opens the box, and inside is the portrait of the old man with the enigmatic gaze. That the painting is authentic there is no doubt, for the newspapers report in banner headlines that the masterpiece at the museum has been stolen.

It's important that the painting be well hidden; the man hangs it in the attic in his mansion, and he is the only one to have a key to that room. There he spends hours looking at the painting, lit by spotlights that he himself has installed. It is with tenderness that he gazes at the face of the old man; he even strokes the wrinkled surface of the canvas with his fingers, moist with perspiration. Merely looking is not enough, he has to touch the painting, too, in order to experience the real feeling of ownership.

The servants wonder about what their master (a childless widower, he lives alone) is up to. But nobody dares ask him a question, and thus, without being disturbed, he can remain in the attic for increasingly longer periods of time. He goes downstairs only for his meals, when he then amuses himself by reading the news in the papers: There are still no clues to the whereabouts of the painting, the chief of police believes it has been taken to New

York. New York! The man laughs, he laughs so hard that he chokes. The servants exchange glances. The man knows that they think him crazy, but he couldn't care less. Now that he has his painting, nothing else matters to him. All he wants is to sit before the old man with the enigmatic gaze. With his brow creased and his lips compressed, the man studies the face in front of him just like an explorer studies the map of the unknown region he is to traverse. The man knows this face thoroughly; at least he thinks he does; however, as soon as he closes his eyes, the face disappears from his memory—completely erased. Which is frustrating, for the face is not as completely his as he imagined it to be; he does not possess it in its entirety. *Once more,* he murmurs, and drawing the chair up closer to the painting, he starts the undertaking anew, trying to memorize the outline of the eyebrows, of the labial commissure, of the wrinkles.

But then—due to the heat of the lights or to moisture, or to some other unknown reason—the painting begins to fade, to vanish. At first the man thinks it is his imagination, an illusion caused by his prolonged effort to engrave in his mind the small details of the portrait. But no, the face is indeed vanishing; day after day the lines keep fading. Inexorably, the painting is vanishing and there is nothing the man can do about it. He cannot consult the experts, he cannot call in the restorers; helpless, he stands rooted before the painting until all that remains of the old man is—for some mysterious reason—his right eye, which glitters, enigmatic. But even this eye vanishes, and one day the man finds himself standing before a blank, empty canvas. And on that day he falls down on his knees; and on that day he weeps as he has not wept since his childhood, and he even calls out to his mother, dead for many years.

The man falls ill. Doctors, several of them, are sent for; they examine him thoroughly, take blood for numerous tests, x-ray him from top to bottom, but they find nothing wrong. His condition deteriorates, the doctors give him up, his death is even announced on television; but, as suddenly as he fell ill, he recovers. The first thing he does after getting rid of the servants, who urge him to stay in bed, is to go upstairs to the attic. Cheered by the hope that everything might have been just delirium, he climbs the steps two at a time. He unlocks the door, turns on the light—and there it is, the blank canvas, before which he sits down, devastated.

Suddenly an idea crosses his mind: And if Jorge were to return the canvas to the museum? It is possible that once there, under the specific circumstances of that environment to which the painting, after all, belongs, the figure will reappear. But why in the world would the museum's curator want to replace a Rafael painting with a blank canvas? And suppose the face were to reappear, what would he do then? Would he have the painting stolen again?

No. No, this is not the right solution. Opening the door— there is no longer any reason to keep it closed—the man calls a servant and dispatches him to a store to buy painting supplies. Later, the man mixes paints, then clumsily wielding the paintbrush, he gives himself over to his work. What he has in mind is just an eye, an enigmatic eye. To begin with. Later, he will see.

INSIDE MY DIRTY HEAD—
THE HOLOCAUST

INSIDE MY DIRTY HEAD, THE HOLOCAUST IS LIKE THIS:

I'm an eleven-year-old boy. Small, skinny. And dirty. Oh boy, am I ever dirty! A stained T-shirt, filthy pants, grimy feet, hands, and face: dirty, dirty. But this external dirt is nothing compared to the filth I have inside my head. I harbor nothing but evil thoughts. I'm mischievous, I use foul language. A dirty tongue, a dirty head. A filthy mind. A sewer inhabited by toads and poisonous scorpions.

My father is appalled. A good man, my father is. He harbors nothing but pure thoughts. He speaks nothing but kind words. Deeply religious; the most religious man in our neighborhood. The neighbors wonder how such a kind, pious man could have such a wicked son with such a bad character. I'm a disgrace to the family, a disgrace to the neighborhood, a disgrace to the world. Me and my dirty head.

My father lost some of his brothers and sisters in the Holocaust. When he talks about this, his eyes well up with tears. It's

5

now 1949; the memories of the World War II are still much too fresh. Refugees from Europe arrive in the city; they come in search of relatives and friends that might help them. My father does what he can to help these unfortunate people. He exhorts me to follow his example, although he knows that little can be expected from someone with such a dirty head. He doesn't know yet what is in store for him. Mischa hasn't materialized yet.

One day Mischa materializes. A diminutive, slightly built man with a stoop; on his arm, quite visible, a tattooed number—the number assigned to him in a concentration camp. He arouses pity, poor fellow. His clothes are in tatters. He sleeps in doorways.

Learning about this distressing situation, my father is filled with indignation: Something must be done about it, one can't leave a Jew in this situation, especially when he is a survivor of the Nazi massacre. He calls the neighbors to a meeting. I want you to attend it, he says to me (undoubtedly hoping that I'll be imbued with the spirit of compassion. I? The kid with the dirty head? Poor Dad).

The neighbors offer to help. Each one will contribute a monthly sum; with this money Mischa will be able to get accommodation in a rooming house, buy clothes, and even go to a movie once in a while.

They announce their decision to the diminutive man who, with tears in his eyes, gushes his thanks. Months go by. Mischa is now one of us. People take turns inviting him to their homes. And they invite him because of the stories he tells them in his broken Portuguese. Nobody can tell stories like Mischa. Nobody can describe like him the horrors of the concentration camp, the filth, the promiscuity, the diseases, the agony of the dying, the brutality of the guards. Listening to him brings tears to everybody's eyes. . . .

Well, not to everybody's. Not to mine. I don't cry. Because of my dirty head, of course. Instead of crying, instead of flinging myself upon the floor, instead of clamoring to heaven as I listen to the horrors he narrates, I keep asking myself questions. Questions like: Why doesn't Mischa speak Yiddish like my parents and everybody else? Why does he stand motionless and silent in the synagogue while everybody else is praying?

Such questions, however, I keep to myself. I wouldn't dare ask anybody such questions; neither do I voice any of the things that my dirty head keeps imagining. My dirty head never rests; day and night, always buzzing, always scheming. . . .

I start imagining this: One day another refugee, Avigdor, materializes in the neighborhood. He, too, comes from a concentration camp; unlike Mischa, however, he doesn't tell stories. And I keep imagining that this Avigdor is introduced to Mischa; and I keep imagining that they detest each other at first sight, even though at one time they were fellow sufferers. I imagine them one night seated at the table in our house; we're having a party, there are lots of people. Then suddenly—a scene that my dirty head has no difficulty devising—suggest that the two men have an arm-wrestling match.

(Why arm wrestling? Why should two puny little men, who in the past almost starved to death, put their strength against each other? Why? Why, indeed? Ask my dirty head why.)

So, there they are, the two men, arm against arm; tattooed arm against tattooed arm; nobody has noticed anything. But I have— thanks, of course, to my dirty head.

The numbers are the same.

"Look," I shout, "the numbers are the same!"

At first, everybody stares at me, bewildered; then they realize what I'm talking about and see for themselves: Both men have the same number.

Mischa has turned livid. Avigdor rises to his feet. He, too, is pale; but his rage soon makes his face and neck break out in red blotches. With unsuspected strength he grabs Mischa by the arm;

he drags him to a bedroom, forces him go to in, then closes the door behind them. Only my dirty head knows what is going on there, for it is my head that has created Avigdor, it is my head that has given Avigdor this extraordinary strength, it is my head that has caused him to open and shut the door; and it is in my head that this door exists. Avigdor is interrogating Mischa, and finding out that Mischa has never been a prisoner anywhere, that he is not even a Jew; he is merely a crafty Ukranian who had himself tattooed and who made up the whole story in order to exploit Jews.

So, once the ruse is exposed, even my dirty head has no difficulty in making Avigdor—and my parents and the neighbors—expel Mischa in a fit of fury. And so Mischa is left destitute, and he has to sleep on a park bench.

My dirty head, however, won't leave him alone, and so I continue to imagine things. With the money Mischa gets from panhandling, he buys a lottery ticket. The number—trust this dirty head of mine to come up with something like this—is, of course, the one tattooed on his arm. And he wins in the lottery! Then he moves to Rio de Janeiro and he buys a beautiful condo and he is happy! Happy. He doesn't know what my dirty head has in store for him.

There's one thing that bothers him though: the number tattooed on his arm. He decides to have it removed. He goes to a famous plastic surgeon (these are refinements devised by my dirty head) and undergoes surgery. But then he goes into shock and dies a slow, agonizing death. . . .

One day Mischa tells my father about the soap bars. He says he saw piles and piles of soap bars in the death camp. Do you know what the soap was made of? he asks. Human fat. Fat taken from Jews.

At night I dream about him. I'm lying naked in something

resembling a bathtub, which is filled with putrid water; Mischa rubs that soap on me; he keeps rubbing it ruthlessly while shouting that he must wash the filth off my tongue and off my head, that he must wash the filth off the world.

I wake up sobbing, I wake up in the midst of great suffering. And it is this suffering that I, for lack of a better word, call the Holocaust.

FIVE ANARCHISTS

THE SECRET SERVICE OF KING IGOR XV HAS CAPTURED FIVE anarchists.

"I'm going to teach those bastards a lesson," the monarch declares to the press.

The five are locked in the same prison cell: Louis Halm, 32, the ringleader; Ruiz Agostin, 38, father of six children; Georges Pompeu, 23, the only son of a widow; Miro Levin, 24, the intellectual of the group, the author of *Anarchy and Independence*; Amedeo Bozzini, 22, the youngest and least experienced.

Ruiz Agostin, on the first day:

"Friends, let's not worry. There's no evidence against us. Soon the king will have to set us free. Cheer up!"

The jailer comes in with the day's ration: five rolls and five mugs of water.

"Is that all?" Amedeo Bozzini protests.

"It's a diet devised by the prison's physician," the jailer replies. "A roll and a mug of water a day will guarantee a person's survival. Enjoy your meal."

The first day goes by, the second goes by, the tenth goes by. The jailer was right: Their hunger is satisfied and they are not undernourished.

To maintain themselves in high spirits, they hold debates:

"The present predicament propritiates . . ."

"Wrong, wrong."

"But the facts of reality . . ."

"Wrong!"

"It's undeniable that . . ."

"You idiot!"

Unfortunately, they begin to lose their temper.

On the twenty-eighth day the guard comes in with four rolls and four mugs of water.

"There's one roll missing," shouts Georges Pompeu.

"And a mug of water!" chimes in Amedeo Bozzini.

"I'm following orders," replies the jailer, and he closes the heavy iron door.

"Friends," says Louis Halm, "we'll survive this trying ordeal. Our solidarity and our faith will help us succeed."

Each one gets four fifths of a roll, and four fifths of a mug of water.

On the following day, it is the same thing; and on the following, and on the following.

At the end of the week their bones begin to show through their skin. Louis Halm calls a meeting.

"Friends," he says in a strained voice, "as we can see, this is killing all of us. It would be better if we sacrificed one of us. Those who remain will wait for freedom, which will be here before long."

"I'd like to volunteer," says Ruiz Agostin.

"No. You've got six kids."

"Me, then," says George Pompeu. "Why not me?"

"Your old mother needs you."

"And who needs me?" asks Miro Levin.

"The people, for you do brainwork for them." A pause, after which Louis Halm goes on. "Everybody is indispensable, but somebody will have to die."

With the help of his companions, Amedeo Bozzini hangs himself from the bars of the jail.

On the following morning the jailer comes in with four rolls and four mugs of water; before leaving, he remarks: "The newspapers are saying that Amedeo has killed himself out of guilt."

"A lie!" shouts Louis Halm.

The jailer shrugs his shoulders, and leaves whistling.

On the fortieth day the ration is once again reduced: three rolls, three mugs of water. The prisoners protest. "I'm following orders," says the jailer.

"Another one of us will have to be sacrificed," says Louis Halm when the jailer is gone.

Ruiz Agostin volunteers again, and so does Georges Pompeu; but this time the chosen one is Miro Levin. "Well, I was really beginning to get tired of being an intellectual," he says before hanging himself.

"The newspapers have reported that Miro Levin was a drug addict," says the jailer on the following morning.

"A lie!" shouts Louis Halm in a weak voice. The jailer leaves.

On the following morning: two rolls, two mugs of water.

"Tell my mother I died for a just cause," Georges Pompeu requests before hanging himself.

On the following morning the jailer remarks: "According to the newspapers, Georges Pompeu's mother will be spitting on her son's grave daily."

Louis Halm and Ruiz Agostin, now reduced to spectral figures, don't even protest.

On the fiftieth day the jailer comes in with one roll and one mug of water.

"Farewell, my friend," says Ruiz Agostin. "I hope you'll soon leave this place to provide leadership to our people. Look after my children!"

Louis Halm helps him hang himself. After ascertaining himself that Ruiz is indeed dead, he goes to the door.

"Hi, there! Jailer!"

The jailer appears.

"That was the last one," says Louis Halm with difficulty. "Go and tell the king that I've carried out my task according to our agreement. And now let me out."

But the jailer stands motionless, blocking the door with his corpulent body.

"Haven't you heard?" says Louis Halm gruffly. "Let me out! And go inform the king. Hurry."

"I've already done so," says the jailer.

"And?"

"He has sent you this."

The jailer produces a tray: one half of a roll. And a mug of water, half filled.

AMONG THE WISE MEN

THEY WENT IN SEARCH OF THE BOY AND FOUND HIM AMONG THE wise men, who were dazzled by this whiz kid.

One wise man:

"What's an abyss?"

"A natural cavity which opens itself in the ground in a roughly vertical way, and whose bottom is practically unexplorable. Next!"

Another wise man:

"And a pyramid? How should we perceive a pyramid?"

"It's a solid figure, limited by a flat polygon ABCD and by the triangles, VAB, VBC, and others, having as a vertex a point V not situated on the plane of the polygon, and as opposite sides all the sides of the polygon. Another wise man, please."

Another wise man:

"And what about Xerxes the First?"

"An Achaemenid king of Persia. He squelched uprisings in Egypt and Chaldea. In the year A.D. 480 he began an expedition into Greece. He fought in the Thermopylae and finally reached Athens. He was defeated in several battles. Another one. Hurry!"

Another wise man hurried forward:

"The opening lines of the *Odyssey*, please."

"Sing to me, O Muse, of the industrious man who, after he sacked the sacred city of Troy, wandered about countless lands, visiting cities and learning the minds of so many men."

And he added peevishly:

"A second-rate question. Is there anyone who can come up with a better question?"

An old man drew near. Respectful but challenging, he asked:

"And what do you have to say about Aristotelian philosophy?"

The boy smiled approvingly yet condescendingly.

"In Platonism, the problem of Oneness is decisive. Aristotle breaks away from this unity, and for this reason he is to be applauded. He has also stated, in his *History of the Animals*, that women have fewer teeth than men. Such a statement is regarded as an aberration. However, I see amazing transcendence in it."

The elders stirred, uneasy; then one of them raised his finger.

"What do you have to say about fish?"

"Provided they are carefully chosen, fish can turn into yummy dishes. But only a fish that has bright, clear eyes, red gills, a well-shaped belly, firm flesh, a pleasant albeit peculiar smell, well-attached scales, and perfect fins. Take this fish. Then scrape the scales off carefully so as not to damage the skin. Gut the fish by slitting the belly open; it's not advisable to pull the guts out through the gills. Then fry it, piece by piece, in some good olive oil. Serve it with round slices of lemon."

Pushing his way to the front of the group, an old man then looked straight at the boy.

"What's the meaning of life?"

At that moment the boy's parents took him away. It was lunchtime. Fish was the main course.

THE CONSPIRACY

WHENEVER A TEACHER WAS ABSENT, DONA MARTA WAS CALLED in as a substitute. She taught singing, a subject regarded as being of secondary importance; besides, her classes were dreadful—but, on the other hand, she was always on call. Mornings, afternoons, evenings. She practically lived in the school. When we arrived in the morning she was already sitting in the staff room, always with that smile of hers, a smile somewhat resigned, somewhat silly; and even after the last of the night-class students had left, she would stay on. Waiting for one of her brothers to pick her up, but since nobody had ever seen this brother, rumor had it that she slept in the attic of the school building. That she had her meals on the premises was certain. At noon she would head for a bench in the school yard, take a sandwich from her bag, and sit munching on it, melancholy.

One day our Portuguese teacher didn't come. Dona Marta was brought in. Entering the classroom in her unsteady gait, she greeted us, then apologized for the absence of her colleague. We wouldn't be singing, she announced, for her voice was hoarse (something difficult to verify, as her voice sounded normally hoarse. Which even gave rise to jibes: Rusty Gullet, we had nicknamed her. Which she ignored, or pretended to ignore).

"We're going to do something different," she said. Then, trying to assume an air of mystery, of complicity: "We'll pretend this is your usual Portuguese class, okay? I'd like you to write a composition. On a topic of your own choice. Then I'll pick five students at random; they'll read their compositions aloud and the best one will win a prize."

She paused, then added: "Here it is."

She took a chocolate bar from her purse. A small, ordinary chocolate bar. And that bar she held up in the air for at least a minute, smiling, happy.

Ours was a school attended by the children of wealthy people. Chocolates, bonbons, candies—we could have them every day, at any time. A chocolate bar? Some of us snickered in derision. But at that moment the school principal appeared at the door and cast a stern look at us. Right away we set to work.

I was sure I wouldn't be called upon to read my composition aloud. I was never called upon to do anything, which suited me fine. This fact, as well as the many mystery books I had been reading at that time, might explain the title of my composition: "The Conspiracy Against the Blind." In it I described a distant country which was ruled by a caste of blind men: a blind king, blind ministers, blind generals—all of them ruthlessly oppressing the people, who couldn't rebel or even conspire: The extremely sharp sense of hearing of the blind detected the slightest muttering of discontent. But even so, determined leaders of the people succeeded in hatching a conspiracy based exclusively on the written word. Books as well as magazines and newspapers denouncing the blind were published. All antiblind thoughts were voiced in writing only. Finally, the oligarchy was overthrown and a new king mounted the throne. His first acts were to destroy all the printing presses, close down the newspapers, and declare literacy illegal.

I finished my composition and sat quietly, waiting. The others were also finishing theirs. "Ready, everybody?" she asked. Everybody said they were. Except me. I kept quiet. But (as ill luck would have it), it was at me that she pointed her hesitant finger.

"You ... what's your name?"

"Oscar," I replied (a lie; my name is Francisco Pedro; I could hear some stifled snickering but I stood firm).

"That's a beautiful name," she said, smiling. "Will you read your composition to us, Oscar?"

There was no way out. I glanced at the sheet of paper, then, after hesitating for a moment, I announced: "I wrote about a walk in the country."

She smiled approvingly. Then I gave an account of a walk in the country. I described the landscape: the trees, the brook, the cattle grazing under a deep blue sky. I concluded by saying that a walk in the country taught us to love nature.

"Very nice," she said when I finished. And she added with emotion: "I'd like to keep your composition."

"It's not worth keeping," I said. "But I'd like to," she persisted. "It's not worth keeping," I repeated. She laughed. "Come on now, Oscar, don't be so modest, let me have your composition."

"This composition belongs to me," I said, "and I can do with it whatever I want. This was supposed to be a singing class, not a Portuguese language class. You have no right to demand anything from me, ma'am."

"I'm asking you for the last time," she said, and her voice was trembling. "I'd like to have your composition. Please."

Taking the sheet of paper, I tore it up amid a sepulchral silence.

She said nothing but all of us could see the tears streaming down her face. Which surprised me: I didn't know then that the blind can cry.

THE PRODIGAL UNCLE

A WEALTHY ENTREPRENEUR SITS IN HIS MANSION WATCHING television with his family when a servant comes in to announce that there is a young man at the door wanting to speak to him.

"He says he's your nephew."

The man gets up and goes to the door, where he finds a plainly dressed youth in his late teens, with an anxious expression on his bearded face. How are you, Uncle, he says; the man hesitates. Who are you? he asks. I'm your nephew Milton, says the youth.

"Milton? You, that little kid?"

"That's me all right, Uncle. Time goes by."

The man opens his arms.

"Here, let's have a hug, Milton!"

The man embraces him for a long time. Then he shows the youth into the room where the family is gathered, and introduces him: Here's the son of my brother João; I hadn't seen him since he was a little boy. Everybody gets up to greet the newcomer;

Aline, the eldest daughter (eighteen years old), smiles shyly. After the greetings, the man asks the youth to sit down by his side on the big sofa and asks him if he has had dinner yet; when the youth replies that he isn't hungry, the man insists that he have something, a whiskey, a beverage; the youth accepts some fruit juice, and while the servant is seeing to it, the man, his eyes bright, turns to the youth.

"Well, now tell me about your parents. I haven't seen them in years."

Whereupon sadness casts a shadow over the youth's face: with his voice cracking, he says that his father is dead and that his mother is in a mental hospital. I didn't know, said the man, dejected. Saying that he was quite fond of his brother, he then reminisces about their childhood days on a small farm full of fruit trees. The conversation drags on; then, noticing that the youth appears to be tired, the man asks him where he is staying; nowhere, is the reply; he has just arrived in town and hasn't found accommodation yet. The man insists that the youth stay at his house. The youth, apparently somewhat reluctant, accepts the invitation. The servant is called to show him to the guest room.

Days go by and the youth stays on. In fact, much to the delight of the family; the entrepreneur's wife enjoys talking to him; the eight-year-old son has found a playmate in him; and Aline, well, Aline is clearly in love. Her parents have noticed, and at the table they exchange glances, smiling.

The entrepreneur offers the youth a job in his company. He accepts. From then on they leave the house together every morning; the young man now dresses in a befitting manner. As a business manager he proves himself to be dynamic, enterprising, intelligent; the entrepreneur's aides are delighted with him. It is predicted that after his engagement to Aline, he will officially take up his duties as executive director.

One night he asks his prospective father-in-law if he can have a word with him. There is a personal matter he would like to discuss. They go to the library; as soon as the entrepreneur closes the door behind them, the young man, on an impulse, kneels down and kisses the entrepreneur's hands. But what's going on, says the man, at once surprised and moved, but the young man, in tears, is too distressed to reply. Finally he calms down, and then he says that he is grateful, very grateful, but not for the reasons the entreprenuer imagines; he is grateful for other, entirely different reasons. The young man then proceeds to tell the entrepreneur that after dropping out of school, he spent a long time loafing around the country, sleeping in shacks and abandoned houses, until he fell in with a group of lawbreakers. Together, they devised a plan to kidnap the entrepreneur and demand a large ransom. Entrusted with this mission, the young man was at first firmly determined to carry it out. Not just for the money; well, for the money, too; but mostly because he believed he would be meting out justice. He carefully studied all the details of the operation. . . .

But the warmth with which he was welcomed, the atmosphere of genuine family love that he found in the house, and also the dynamism, the intelligence, the kindness of the entrepreneur—all of this (contrasting so sharply with the erroneous ideas about businessmen that the youth used to have) caused a change of heart. Renouncing violence, he now wants to forget the past and turn over a new leaf. I realize, he says, that I was living before in a world of fanatical fantasies, in a world of dangerous illusions; thank goodness, I withdrew in time, before I turned into a criminal. All I want now is to build a home full of love and comfort for my wife and children. I owe my good intentions to you, sir. I'll never forget the lesson in life that I've learned here, a lesson for which I'll be grateful to you forever.

The entrepreneur listens in silence. But you're really my nephew, aren't you? he finally asks. The young man hesitates; he hesitates for a long time before saying that he made up the whole story. He used to know the entrepreneur's real nephew; from that youth, later killed in an accident, he obtained all the information he needed to pose as the entrepreneur's nephew.

Then the entrepreneur rises to his feet, says he has some matter to attend to, and asks the young man to wait in the library. He leaves. Ten minutes later he returns, accompanied by two of his security guards. Arrest this man, he says dryly. The young man looks at him with disbelief, horror even; slowly, however, a smile begins to open his face. Thank you, Uncle, he says at last. After kissing the man's hands once more, he leaves, escorted by the guards.

ROOT CANAL TREATMENT

STILL DIZZY FROM THE DRONE OF THE DENTIST'S DRILL, AND WITH part of her face frozen, she left the dentist's office and walked toward the elevator. Wanting above anything else at that moment to get home and lie down, she pressed the button.

A man stood there, waiting for the elevator. Partly because she wasn't feeling well, and partly because the corridor—notwithstanding the fancy building—was poorly lit, it wasn't until several seconds later that she noticed his presence. The man was still young and—a detail that didn't escape her—relatively well dressed. Had he been raggedly dressed and, on top of that, evil-looking, she wouldn't of course have stayed there for another moment and would have hastily sought refuge in the dentist's office. But no, nothing in the man's appearance roused distrust. So, she looked at her watch—six o'clock in the evening—and pressed the elevator button again.

Suddenly the man let out a moan, staggered, and leaned against the wall. Startled, she looked at him. Startled and annoyed. That's all she needed, to have to help a stranger when she herself could barely stand on her own two legs. She wanted to ignore him; she wished she could. But no, it wasn't in her to ignore other people. For which she often censured herself: I'm always taking care of others, I'm neglectful of myself, a patsy, that's what I am. She looked around; her last hope was for someone to appear and take charge of the case (if it was indeed a case; everything seemed to indicate that it was; the man seemed really ill). But no, nobody appeared. Only the two of them in the long corridor. God's will be done, she thought. She addressed the man.

"Aren't you feeling well?"

He looked at her. He wasn't ugly; he wasn't good-looking, either. A man with an ordinary face—like her own, as a matter of fact (I have an ordinary face, she was in the habit of whispering as she looked at herself in the mirror at night; an ordinary face, an ordinary life).

"What?" The voice was weak, a child's voice, almost.

"I asked if you weren't feeling well."

"If I'm not feeling well . . . ?" He looked at her as if he hadn't understood. "If I'm not feeling well . . . ? I don't know. I think I'm not feeling well. Yes, I'm sick. I have cancer."

"Gosh," she murmured. She didn't know what to say. To her own indisposition was now added the discomfiture created by this situation; a horrible situation. And to make matters worse, the elevator wouldn't come.

Fortunately, the man seemed to be rallying. Taking a deep breath, he pulled a handkerchief out of his pocket and mopped his forehead.

"Cancer," he said. "The doctor said there's no doubt about it. He's quite frank. One of those that will hold nothing back from you, you know. You have cancer, my friend, you're not going to live much longer, you'd better set your affairs in order."

Poor man, she thought. Poor, poor man. Suddenly she was struck by remorse—what was her root canal compared to this man's cancer?—and at the same time by relief: root canal was preferable to cancer. Anything would be preferable to cancer. Not that she was safe from cancer, of course; all it takes for a person to fall ill is to be alive, but it wasn't her turn yet; no, it wasn't. At that moment it fell to her lot to suffer from a tooth infection; at that moment she was safe; in that corridor, with the two of them, Death had drawn lots and the lot fell upon the man. *Not my turn yet.* Relieved, she felt generous, ready to offer help.

"Is there anything I can do?"

The man raised his head, and looked at her again, as if only at that moment he had become aware of the presence of another person, of a woman.

"You ..."

He hesitated. Of course. Confronted with his own death, how could a man not hesitate? This confrontation gave him the right to say whatever he wanted—which he wouldn't do under other circumstances (perhaps because of his upright character). This confrontation gave him the right to ask, to demand, anything from any person, from any woman. For the time being, he still hesitated, but despair would break down barriers and overcome scruples, and he would end up by making her a propostion which, he imagined, was on his mind, as it was on the mind of every other man, good or bad, healthy or dying. He would end up by inviting her to go to a motel with him. And she wouldn't be able to recoil, offended, from a proposition that was, after all, merely normal; a proposition that any man, even if stricken by cancer, or for this very reason, could make to any woman, no matter how straitlaced she was, for the very reason that he was near the end, near the stopping point of a countdown now measured in months, perhaps days, hours. And what would she say, then, to get out of this situation? But, my friend, I don't even know you, we haven't been introduced—would she say that? Would that do as an excuse? This banal line, this stock phrase with which she warded off brash males (who, in fact, were growing scarcer as her youth retreated)? But he wasn't a brash male, nor was he an opportunist. Or, if he was an opportunist, he had every right to be one. I'm a virgin—would she say that? Could she use as an argument the very thing she now regarded as a stigma, a sign of her inability to live? No. There was nothing she could say. The man would invite her to go to a motel and she would have to accompany him, the two of them marching, on their respective paths, toward the gallows.

Just then the elevator came.

Mumbling a vague *good-bye*, she rushed headlong into the elevator, settled herself amid the other people, then stood still and shaky. It wasn't until the doors closed that she realized that the man hadn't followed her. The elevator slowly went down: 12, 11, 10 . . . The man had remained up there. In the gloomy corridor.

At the front door she stopped and peered outside. A street in the downtown area of a big city, a busy street—people, cars, motorbikes. On the facade of the store across the street, the lights of a neon sign went on and out. CORA FASHIONS, CORA FASHIONS. My God, she thought, what have I done? I've run away from a sick man, a man in need of help; it was fear that has made me run away—but fear of what, when he didn't harm me?

No, she couldn't accept this. Her self-dignity wouldn't let her. She had behaved like a coward, like a frightened rat; she had behaved like a fool. But there was still time to right her fault. All she had to do was to return to the fourteenth floor, speak to the man, justify herself (she could say something like I thought you were going to take the elevator, too. Any explanation would do), ask again if she could be of any help, and then, yes, say a friendly good-bye. She went back to the elevator; when the doors opened, she hesitated again; then the doors began to close—but at the very last moment she managed to leap in. *That was a bit of luck!* she thought. Was it, really? (That doubt, again. Again and forever: doubt, indecision, fear.) Should I go back? Won't I get involved in a mess? She was annoyed at herself: A mess? What mess? A mess, why? There won't be any mess. She would simply speak to the man, justify herself with a carefully prepared excuse, then politely say to him: Would the *senhor* (*senhor?* Why not *você* or *tu*, the informal way of addressing a person? No. No familiarities—even taking into account the man's predicament; even taking into account her possible earlier rudeness to him. *Você?* No. Nor *tu*. Later, perhaps—but when would this later be? Would there be any time left for "later"? Did she want it? Questions, questions.) please finish what you were saying before?

The elevator stopped. The doors opened. She stepped out, looked to this side, to that side. Nobody. The corridor was deserted.

It occurred to her that the man might have returned to his doctor's office: Maybe he was really feeling ill, maybe he was feeling even worse now. Anyhow, she thought, if he had decided to see his doctor again, then this matter is no longer in my hands. However, she had to admit to herself that she was disappointed; frustrated; distressed even; on the verge of tears. It would be nice if everything could be solved once and for all.

The door to the doctor's office was open; this fact struck her as a sign, an encouraging sign, so, she decided to make another attempt. She would go in; if she found the man in the waiting room, she would ask him if everything was all right; then, regardless of the answer, or the connotations or veiled propositions of the answer, she would consider the case closed, say good-bye, and leave.

But she didn't see the man in the waiting room. The doctor

and the receptionist were there, both getting ready to leave. Can I help you? asked the receptionist politely. No, she replied, embarrassed, I must have entered the wrong room, sorry. She hurried out.

She was feeling sick now, so sick that she had to lean against the wall: dizzy, nauseated, sick, sick. What in the world made me come back? she kept asking herself. Why didn't I go straight home?

The elevator came. It wasn't the one she had taken before. Then it occurred to her: While I was going up, he was going down—such things do happen. Things that are funny in the movies.

With a faint, absurd hope, she stepped out of the elevator. Maybe the man was still somewhere in that area: standing at the main entrance, for instance; he could well be watching the neon sign and be pondering on the significance of the lights going on and off; or he could be watching the street, the passersby, the cars.

No, the man wasn't there. As she reached the main entrance, she looked to this side, then looked to that side. She didn't see him among the people walking by. Or in the cars parked on the street. Or anywhere.

She hailed a taxi. She got in and gave the driver her destination. Normally, she would have taken the bus; although she earned a relatively good salary, she tried to save. At the moment, however, she felt she was in no condition to stand on a bus line.

They drove in silence. After a remark or two about the weather—it's been very hot, it's going to rain—the taxi driver fell silent. They arrived at the neighborhood where she lived; three blocks before her street, she asked the taxi driver to stop, and she got out of the car. She wanted to walk for a while. But walking didn't dispel the anxiety she had been feeling. Perhaps she should have walked a longer distance. Perhaps: too late now.

At home, her mother was waiting for her; worried, of course. Her mother worried about everything. I was delayed at the dentist's, she said. She couldn't tell her mother about the incident with the man; she wished she could; she wished she could talk to her mother more openly; her mother was the only person she had, now that her sisters were living far away, one in Rio, the other in Recife. But her mother got upset easily; sometimes she would lose sleep over a movie she had watched on television, and would have to take sleeping pills. So, she merely made a remark about something or other—it's hot, isn't it?—then went to the kitchen to get dinner ready. This was something her mother couldn't do because of her arthritis. There was hardly anything her mother could still do. So, she had to do the cooking, run the household, and look after everything. But she didn't complain. She did all the work and didn't complain.

The effect of the anesthetic was wearing off, and she was feeling better; but she couldn't stop thinking about the man. She was annoyed at herself. The matter is closed, I should have spoken to him but didn't, now there's nothing that can be done, and if there's no solution to a problem, the problem is thus solved.

She didn't eat much. Her mother noticed. You didn't each much, she said. It's the tooth, she explained. Does it hurt? asked the mother, alarmed—everything was cause for alarm: the flu, a headache. No, Mother, it doesn't hurt, but the dentist told me not to chew on this side. She waited until her mother finished eating, then she cleared the table and did the dishes. Later they sat down to watch some television. At ten o'clock she bade her mother good night and went to bed.

Naturally, she found herself unable to sleep. The image of the man haunted her; in particular, his beseeching eyes. Tossing about in bed, she cursed herself, she could have prevented all of this, she could have made the dental appointment for some other day, but no, she had insisted on this day because business at the office happened to be slow; and now she was paying for her insistence, for her compulsion to do the right thing. Everything right: everything wrong. As usual.

It was hot; she was drenched in sweat. I need a shower, she murmured. Sometimes she would get up in the middle of the night to take a shower. An adventure, in a way. Innocuous, but still an adventure. She jumped out of bed, and after ascertaining herself that her mother was asleep, she went to the bathroom. She stood a long time under the tepid shower, which normally had a wholesome effect on her, as if the water, cleansing her mind, carried her torments down the drain. Now, however, it was impossible for her to relax; because of the man, of course. She seemed to see him there, in the bathroom, looking at her desperately. She closed her eyes tightly; and suddenly she wished she were ill. She wished she had cancer. Not something annihilating, terminal cancer; a modest tumor, which would be able to soak up her anxiety like a sponge soaks up water. She would like to have the opportunity to be cut up; to suffer pain; to have a big, conspicuous scar. She began to palpate her belly, her neck, her breasts (which no other hand, except the hand of her female gynecologist, had ever touched)—nothing. Just the usual flesh, fat, tendons. The same ones with which she had been endowed at birth, and which she had nourished with sandwiches and fruit juices; and a skin that was now beginning to turn flaccid. Grabbing the towel, she dried herself vigorously, then put on her nightgown and went back to bed. She fell into a doze, woke up, then dozed off again, dreaming about entangled, anguishing things. With relief she saw the day dawn.

She got up early, washed, got dressed, had a cup of black coffee. Flipping through the newspaper, she lingered over the announcements of deaths. Mário Mendes, could that be him? Francisco (Chico) Westdorfer? Dr. Armando Fonseca? How could she know? She couldn't even recall the man's face, she discovered, feeling uneasy. That's how flighty she was. Grabbing her purse, she went out. The bus took a long time to come, and she was late for work. Berenice, the other secretary, was already in the office. Beautiful, charming, and elegant as usual, Berenice wanted to know if everything had been all right at the dentist's. Yes, she replied, everything went well. She couldn't tell the other woman about the man in the corridor. She wouldn't understand. A free, emancipated woman, Berenice lived alone; she had several boyfriends and took turns going to bed with each one of them; and she never missed the chance to rebuke her fellow worker: You keep blaming yourself for things that aren't your fault.

She sat down at the typewriter—and couldn't help thinking again: Even this shows how different our situations are. In this export company where they both worked, Berenice, a bilingual secretary, was responsible for typing the letters in English, and for this reason she had a better quality typewriter, an electronic Olivetti. She, however, had an ordinary typewriter on which she typed the letters in Portuguese. But she refused to ask for a better one, despite Berenice's insistence that she do so: I really like this typewriter, it was on a similar one that I learned how to type.

The man. What was he doing now, the poor man? Was he at his home? At work, trying to keep his mind off death, now near (how near?)? Already in the hospital? Already?

At lunch in a luncheonette, she couldn't eat a thing. What's the matter? asked Berenice. It's my tooth, she lied, it hurts a little. Why don't you go back to that lady dentist of yours, said Berenice, she'll have to do something about it. Go, I'll look after the office.

That's how Berenice was—bossy, determined. Which rather annoyed her, for she thought that Berenice meddled too much in her life. But now an idea struck her: Yes, she would go back—

not to the dentist's office, but to the doctor's office. She would pour out her heart to the doctor; she would talk about the man she had met in the corridor, speak to him of her remorse, ask him to help her find the man. Undoubtedly, the doctor would show sympathy for her; doctors are trained to be sympathetic to people.

Upon returning to the office, she consulted the telephone directory and found the doctor's phone number. Before dialing, she hesitated: Should I or shouldn't I? She dialed the number. The receptionist answered. Yes, the doctor was in, but only for a short time; he had come to the office just to pick up some papers for the income tax people. Please, she whispered, ask him if he can see me. The receptionist said she would speak to the doctor. Minutes went by, long minutes they were, before finally the receptionist came back on the phone. The doctor said he'll see you but you'll have to come right away.

Quickly grabbing her purse and her coat, she said to Berenice, I'm leaving now, I'm going to the dentist.

And suddenly she is hit by an urge, a great urge, to hurry away: she runs out of the building, hails a taxi, gets into the car, tells the taxi driver to head for downtown. The cabbie—young, handsome, and garrulous—talks nonstop about politics, about soccer, about the heat. But what am I doing, she wonders, what in the world am I doing? She's on her way to the doctor, she'll tell him an entangled, crazy story, what will the doctor think of her? And yet the taxi is already in the downtown area; she's getting closer and closer to the final catastrophe.

They arrive. She pays, gets some change back, but doesn't alight from the taxi. What is she hoping for? Is she hoping that the taxi driver will guess at her dilemma? That he will offer to help her? That he will declare himself in love, I love you, ma'am, let's go to a motel right away? I can't stop here, says the man, already impatient at the delay, would you mind getting out quickly, ma'am? She gets out, the taxi speeds away, the tires screeching on the asphalt.

For a moment she stands still. She sighs, then heads for the entrance of the building, goes in, and walks down the long corridor. The elevator is there, its doors open. She steps in, presses a button, the doors close, and there she is, slowly ascending in a closed compartment, immersed in the brightness of the fluorescent lights. She gets out of the elevator, takes a few hesitant steps, stops. In front of her is the door to the doctor's office. Some time ago she devised a plan, which consisted in her going in there and telling this man, this doctor, about something that had happened to her. But she can't carry out this plan. She just can't. The absurdity paralyzes her.

Suddenly her tooth starts to hurt.

With growing elation she realizes this fact: Her tooth hurts. A pain that grows by the minute, an excruciating pain; a pain that, triumphant, imposes itself; a pain that immobilizes her, that galvanizes her. With simple but genuine joy she receives the good news—the pain; it is the answer to all her anxieties; better yet, it makes answers unnecessary. In the canal of her tooth another creature is in a period of gestation—herself, in the process of being reborn. Her old carcass will burst open, and here in this corridor, resurrection will take place. Slivers of light dance before her eyes; she turns around, and like an automaton, she advances toward the dentist's office. She doesn't have an appointment for today, but what does she care? Whoever is in pain has rights. She opens the door and walks in. With her head held high.

THE INTERPRETER

WHEN I ARRIVE, THEY ARE ALREADY SEATED AT THE TABLE—
the father, the mother, the son. But they haven't started dinner
yet; they're waiting for me. I'm late. I've walked all the way here.

On my arrival, their heads rise briskly. The father's gray. The
mother's, gray, too, despite the hair tint. The youth's, shaved (it is,
I know, a form of protest). The eyeglasses—all three wear them—
glitter in the strong electric lights, hiding their eyes and whatever
they might be expressing—anger, or fear, or sorrow, or even
hope.

They—the father and the mother—rise and walk up to me.
We exchange greetings and remarks about the weather. This
winter has been awful, says the mother, it makes people feel
under the weather. I agree; her eyes are congested; it could be
from crying, but it could also be from a cold. One shouldn't
dramatize. I say good evening to the youth, who mutters something in reply and remains seated, motionless. I put my hand on
his shoulder: It's a friendly gesture. A buzzer sounds in the

pantry, which adjoins the dining room. The button is under the table; while the mother was sitting down again, she pressed it with her foot, thus summoning the maid. The family enjoys all the comforts of life; the father, a prosperous sales representative, can afford to provide his family with all the amenities, if not luxuries, of life. The maid that appears at the door wears a cap and a starched apron; and the soup tureen that she brings in is made of porcelain. But when the father eats the first spoonful, the slurping noise betrays his humble origins which, incidentally, he doesn't repudiate: I started from nothing, he often says with pride. The son, however, makes a grimace of disgust. His father's table manners annoy him. He can't stand the boorishness of the bourgeois.

Good soup, I remark with joviality. I'm forty-two years old, and I live alone (I'm considered a weird, albeit charming, bachelor), but even so I maintain my sense of humor and I know how to look straight at life with one eye ironic, the other tender; with one eye mirthful, the other serene. I'm a judicious man; this couple—my cousin and his wife—know this. That's why they keep inviting me over for dinner. They know I won't let silence descend upon this table. To let silence envelop them like dense, dark magma? Unthinkable. I'm a geology professor (currently unemployed; this dinner, by the way, is very timely, it's the first decent meal I've had in many months); but I know that such things upset people. Before I'm through with the soup, I have time to comment on three different things:

—a movie depicting the facetious side of life, recently shown in the movie theaters of the capital city;

—the playoffs in the soccer championship;

—a modular stereo system consisting of a receiver, a record player, and a tape deck (which I'm hoping they'll give me as a birthday gift).

To my first comment the youth reacts by merely raising his

head, without displaying any further interest; to the second, ditto; to the third he reacts by smiling, for I'm now telling them about my outrageous experience with a stereo system—I wanted to tune in to an FM station, but instead I somehow triggered the tone arm of the turntable, which then kept joggling back and forth like a crazy turkey. Like a crazy turkey! I repeat, hitting the table with my fist and roaring with laughter. The youth smiles.

The salad is brought in and for one full minute—but not exceeding one—we munch in silence on the leaves of lettuce and on the round slices of cucumber. The dressing is superb—at once mild and peppery—and I say, The dressing is superb, Cousin. Grateful, she smiles.

Next comes the main course: roast beef garnished with peas, carrots, and french fries, everything topped with a remoulade sauce. Before I start helping myself, the father leans toward me: *Ask him,* he murmurs, *how things are.* The moment has come!

Laying down my knife and fork, I pick up my napkin. After wiping my mouth carefully, I turn to the youth.

"So, young man, how are things?"

He doesn't look at me. He's cutting the meat, and, still cutting it, he replies: Everything's fine, everything's the same.

The mother lifts her napkin to her eyes. It's not the most suitable kind of fabric—the napkin is stiff with starch—with which to wipe tears, but she doesn't have a handkerchief handy; it seems that tears have taken her by suprise in the course of this dinner. But it's a fleeting emotion; before long, she heaves a sigh and mumbles something. Unintelligible words addressed to everybody, or to nobody, or to me, or to God, or to her son, or even to the maid, although she isn't in the room at the moment.

Once again the father leans toward me. *Ask him,* he says in a tense, quite audible voice, *if he has changed his mind.*

I'd say he hasn't, it doesn't seem to me that the youth has

changed his mind; but it doesn't behoove me to have an opinion. My cousin wants me to ask the question, so I ask.

"Well, my lad, have you changed your mind?"

Although he doesn't reply, it's obvious that his mind is made up. He's leaving. Soon. Tomorrow. Or tonight. Maybe after dinner. Maybe he won't even finish dinner.

The father is terrified. He doesn't know what happened, or what's happening, or what will happen. He knows nothing, he doesn't even know how to talk. Shaking, he leans toward me once more: *Ask him what he wants,* he whispers, *in order to change his mind.*

I take a sip of wine, then put the glass down. I won't make my cousin's words mine; I find them unsuitable. The proposition may even be sound, but the way it has been presented is totally wrong. I have a better way.

"Isn't it possible, perhaps," I say in a casual tone, "that on second thought you might change your mind?"

I wait for several seconds before adding: "Isn't there anything that could perhaps make you change your mind?"

"Shit!" he cries out, throwing his napkin aside and rising to his feet. "Shit! Can't people even eat in peace?"

Then the worst happens: The father and the mother get up and start to scream and to cry, and the mother, like a madwoman, starts to pull at her hair. For a few seconds the son looks at them full of hatred, of despair, of bitterness. Then he walks out.

Devastated, the two of them let themselves collapse on their chairs. With a mingle of despair and accusation, the father looks at me: Why don't you do something? But there's nothing I can do now. However, I want to show them that life goes on; with this intention, I cut a piece of meat, stuff it into my mouth, and chew vigorously. "Scrumptious, this roast beef!" I say with my mouth full.

Even though there's something missing, hmm? There's something missing. There's a certain emptiness inside me, an emptiness that can't be filled with meat or peas or wine—it will take this one specific thing to fill it, such a plain and delicious thing whose name escapes me at the moment. My mouth opens but no sound comes out; I raise my hand, make a gesture, point to it—but I can't remember the name of this thing, which is so good, of this thing whose image is so clear to me: a slightly crisp crust, with a soft, fragrant, warm core. The name suddenly pops into my mind and, joyful, I cry out as they, stunned, stare at me, as if I were speaking in that language of the yellow race:

"Bread!"

ATLAS

1

It fell to the giant Atlas's lot to support the world upon his back, a task that had been assigned to him by—whom? He no longer remembered. By whom, and why, and when, he no longer remembered. Neither did he know when he would be relieved of this duty, or when he would be replaced. All he knew was that he had to support the world and there he remained, motionless, on his knees, stooping under the weight of the globe. Without complaining, without seeking help from anyone. As a matter of fact, nobody would ever offer him help. Younger and stronger, the other giants didn't commiserate with him on his fate at all; what's more, they would even reproach Atlas for his alleged arrogance: Did he then see himself as being very important? Did he think of his job as being exceptional?

"The Earth! It's not even one of the biggest planets!"

They were wrong. Atlas was unpretentious. And he didn't even look upon what he did as labor. Labor? Certainly not. Now, if he were carrying the Earth from one universe to the next, if

40

he were shifting it, say, one meter, even one millimeter, then yes, one could consider this labor. But no, Atlas was always motionless, frozen still, and for this reason he kept reproaching himself day in, day out, year in, year out: *I'm a bum, I'm a bum.* He envied those who roamed across the skies, taming comets or rekindling the flame of the stars—tasks that demanded great skill, if not virtuosity. But he did nothing, and there was no call for any skills. A rock could replace him. A giant tortoise. Four elephants.

And yet his was a hard, arduous responsibility. The mountain ranges bruised his shoulders; the tropical rain forests irritated his neck, giving him a rash; and once a peninsula had penetrated the auricle of his ear, causing a serious infection. Just think how much worse it would be if you had to carry the sun, his wife would say, trying to comfort him. Atlas had to admit that she was right. At least the Earth was cool, except for the occasional eruption of a volcano, when he would receive second- or third-degree burns.

2

Atlas rarely slept. Sometimes he managed to have a nap. And in those moments he would dream about the inhabitants of his planet: tiny creatures whom he had never seen, but he imagined that, smiling, they waved at him from their tiny houses or from their tiny ships. On waking up, he would try to forget those dreams. There was no way he could substantiate them; this impossibility depressed him, and it accounted for the sadness on his face and the vacant gaze of his eyes, lost in the infinity.

3

The wife of the giant Atlas was a bitter woman. She envied her friends, whose husbands had interesting jobs and earned decent wages. My husband, she would write in her diary, has a weird occupation for which he doesn't get paid. She would turn to knitting for comfort.

As for his children, they were pranksters. Seeing Atlas stooping under the weight of the world, they would tickle him in the armpits. And they would laugh, they would split their sides with laughter. Atlas would have loved to join in the laughter, too. However, were he to do so, he would run the risk of dropping the world, a catastrophe of unpredictable consequences. For Atlas, being tickled was a really unbearable torture. All his muscles would contract in his effort to remain motionless; beads of sweat would gather on his forehead; tears would stream down his face. But even so, he would wear a fixed wooden smile, a smile that was almost a grimace—until the children, bored by their own pranks, would go away.

4

On a certain Saturday, Charles Atlas took his children to the zoo. While they were running through the graveled alleys, he stood admiring a lion. The feline was dozing. Or perhaps, treacherously, it was just pretending to be asleep, because all of a sudden it opened its eyes. For a few seconds they—the man and the beast—stared at each other; the puny man and the magnificent beast. Then the lion stretched its limbs. My God, thought Charles Atlas, its muscles run under its skin like bunnies running under a carpet! And the lion isn't even doing calisthenics or lifting weights, it's merely exercising its willpower. An animal's willpower, infinitely weaker than the will of a rational human being like me!

He felt he was on the verge of making a major discovery—a method using self-control by which it would be possible for him to develop powerful muscular masses in his arms, in his legs, in his abdomen, even in his scalp. He would become as strong as—a lion! A tiger? Much stronger than a lion or a tiger! He wouldn't have to put up with his boss's insults anymore. And, by teaching his method to others, he would become rich. He would be able to bedeck his wife with jewels and to afford expensive toys for his children.

Shouts of distress aroused him from his thoughts. He turned around, his children were nowhere in sight. A small crowd had gathered in front of the tigers' cage. Running to it, he elbowed his way through the crowd—and he couldn't contain a scream of horror. His younger daughter had managed to squeeze herself through the bars of the cage and there she stood now, among the beasts. Charles Atlas took a step forward and fell to the ground, unconscious.

When he came to, the little girl stood in front of him, looking at him curiously. She had come out of the cage with the same boldness that had prompted her in. Weeping, Charles Atlas threw himself at her.

He bought his children popcorn and ice cream; he loaded them with popcorn and ice cream. Then he took them to the amusement park, and he spent all his money, down to the last cent—what did it matter?—on the the children. At nightfall they returned home, Charles Atlas carrying the tyke on his shoulders. He wasn't loaded down with her weight; she wasn't a burden at all.

His wife, worried about their delay, greeted them. You'll have to be up early tomorrow, she reminded him. True: On the following day Atlas would have to resume his usual task of carrying the world on his back.

But he didn't go to bed. He sat down on a chair in the living room, and there he remained, smoking in the dark. He was envisioning a new method for developing muscles. A method that would make him strong, rich, famous. One day, he was thinking, I'll hold the world in the palm of my hand.

A BRIEF HISTORY OF CAPITALISM

MY FATHER WAS A COMMUNIST AND A CAR MECHANIC. A GOOD Communist, according to his comrades, but a lousy mechanic according to consensus. As a matter of fact, so great was his inability to handle cars that people wondered why he had chosen such an occupation. He used to say it had been a conscious choice on his part; he believed in manual work as a form of personal development, and he had confidence in machines and in their capability to liberate man and launch him into the future, in the direction of a freer, more desirable life. Roughly, that's what he meant.

I used to help my father in his car repair shop. Since I was an only son, he wanted me to follow in his footsteps. There wasn't, however, much that I could do; at that time I was eleven years old, and almost as clumsy as he was at using tools. Anyhow, for the most part, there was no call for us to use them since there wasn't much work coming our way. We would sit talking and thus while away the time. My father was a great storyteller;

enthralled, I would listen to his accounts of the uprising of the Spartacists, and of the rebellion led by the fugitive slave Zambi. In those moments his eyes would glitter. I would listen, deeply affected by his stories; often, my eyes would fill with tears.

Once in awhile a customer appeared. Usually a Party sympathizer (my father's comrades didn't own cars), who came to Father more out of a desire to help than out of need. These customers played it safe, though: It was always some minor repair, like fixing the license plate securely, or changing the blades of the windshield wipers. But even such simple tasks turned out to be extraordinarily difficult for Father to perform; sometimes it would take him a whole day to change a distributor point. And the car would drive away with the engine misfiring (needless to say, its owner would never set foot in our repair shop again). If it weren't for the financial problems (my mother had to support us by taking in sewing), I wouldn't have minded the lack of work too much. I really enjoyed those rap sessions with my father. In the morning I would go to school; but as soon as I came home, I would run to the repair shop, which was near our house. And there I would find Father reading. Upon my arrival, he would set his book aside, light his pipe, and start telling me his stories. And there we would stay until Mother came to call us for dinner.

One day when I arrived at our repair shop, there was a car there, a huge, sparkling, luxury car. None of the Party sympathizers, not even the wealthiest among them, owned a car like that. Father told me that the monster car had stalled right in front of the shop. The owner then left it there, under his care, saying he would be back late in the afternoon. And what's wrong with it? I asked, somewhat alarmed, sensing a foul-up in the offing.

"I wish I knew." Father sighed. "Frankly, I don't know what's wrong with it. I already took a look but couldn't find the defect.

It must be something minor, probably the carburetor is clogged up, but . . . I don't know, I just don't know what it is."

Dejected, he sat down, took a handkerchief out of his pocket, and wiped his forehead. Come on, I said, annoyed at his passivity, it's no use your sitting there.

He got up and the two of us took a look at the enormous engine, so clean, it glittered. Isn't it a beauty? remarked my father with the pleasure of an owner who took pride in his car.

Yes, it was a beauty—except that he couldn't open the carburetor. I had to give him a hand; three hours later, when the man returned, we were still at it.

He was a pudgy, well-dressed man. He got out of a taxi, his face already displaying annoyance. I expected him to be disgruntled, but never for a moment did I imagine what was to happen next.

At first the man said nothing. Seeing that we weren't finished yet, he sat down on a stool and watched us. A moment later he stood up; he examined the stool on which he had sat.

"Dirty. This stool is dirty. Can't you people even offer your customers a decent chair to sit on?"

We made no reply. Neither did we raise our heads. The man looked around him.

"A real dump, this place. A sty. How can you people work amid such filth?"

We, silent.

"But that's the way everything is," the man went on. "In this country that's the way it is. Nobody wants to do any work, nobody wants to get his act together. All people ever think of is booze, women, the Carnival, soccer. But to get down to work? Never."

Where's the wrench? asked Father in a low, restrained voice. Over there, by your side, I said. Thanks, he said, and resumed fiddling with the carburetor.

"You people want nothing to do with a regular, steady job."
The man sounded increasingly more irritated. "You people will
never get out of this filth. Now, take me, for instance. I started at
the bottom. But nowadays I'm a rich man. Very rich. And do
you know why? Because I was clean, well organized, hardworking.
This car here, do you think it's the only one I own? Do you?"

Tighten the screw, said Father, tighten it really tight.

"I'm talking to you!" yelled the man, fuming. "I'm asking you
a question! Do you think this is the only car I own? That's what
you think, isn't it? Well, let me tell you something, I own two
other cars. Two other cars! They are in my garage. I don't use
them. Because I don't want to. If I wanted, I could abandon this
car here in the middle of the street and get another one. Well, I
wouldn't get it myself; I would have someone get it for me.
Because I have a chauffeur, see? That's right. I drive because I
enjoy driving, but I have a chauffeur. I don't *have* to drive, I
don't *need* this car. If I wanted to, I could junk this fucking car,
you hear me?"

Hand me the pipe wrench, will you? said Father. The small
one.

The man was now standing quite close to us. I didn't look at
him, but I could feel his breath on my arm.

"Do you doubt my word? Do you doubt that I can smash up
this car? Do you?"

I looked at the man. He was upset. When his eyes met mine,
he seemed to come to his senses; only for a moment, though; he
opened his eyes wide.

"Do you doubt it? That I can smash up this fucking car? Give
me a hammer. Quick! Give me a hammer!"

He searched for a hammer but couldn't find one (it would
have been a miracle had he found one; even we could never find
the tools in our shop). Without knowing what he was doing, he
gave the car door a kick; soon followed by another, then another.

"That's what I've been telling you," he kept screaming. "That I'll smash up this fucking car! That's what I've been telling you."

Ready, said Father. I looked at him; he was pale, beads of sweat were running down his face. Ready? I asked, not getting it. Ready, he said. You can now start the engine.

The man, panting, was looking at us. Opening the car door, I sat at the steering wheel and turned on the ignition. Incredible: The engine started. I revved it up. The shop was filled with the roar of the engine.

My father stood mopping his face with his dirty handkerchief. The man, silent, kept looking at us. How much I owe you? finally he asked. Nothing, said my father. What do you mean, nothing? Suspicious, the man frowned. Nothing, said my father, it costs you nothing, it's on the house. Then the man, opening his wallet, pulled out a bill.

"Here, for a shot of rum."

"I don't drink," said my father without touching the money.

The man replaced the bill in his wallet, which he then put into his pocket. Without a word he got into his car, and, revving the engine, drove away.

For a moment Father stood motionless, in silence. Then he turned to me.

"This," he said in a hoarse voice, a voice that wasn't his, "is capitalism."

No, it wasn't. That wasn't capitalism. I wished it were capitalism—but it was not. Unfortunately not. It was something else. Something I didn't even dare to think about.

A PUBLIC ACT

RECENTLY, IN BRUSSELS, A PUBLIC ACT WAS STAGED AS A PROTEST against the arms race and the armed conflicts that keep erupting in various points of the globe. The event took place in an auditorium, which wasn't very big, but it was filled to capacity. Speaker after speaker took to the podium, and particularly vehement was the last speaker, a highly respected physics professor who described at length the horrors of an atomic war. While the old professor was speaking, a man in the second row stood up, walked up to the podium, then, in front of the stunned audience, he drew a gun and fired five shots at the professor, who fell down.

The incident created panic and confusion, with everybody wanting to leave; but suddenly the man shouted: "Wait! Wait a moment!"

The audience turned to the podium: There he was, and at his side, smiling, stood the professor. The man then explained that the whole thing had been just an act—blank cartridges had been

used in order to give the audience a dramatic, therefore didactic,
demonstration of the savage and treacherous tactics of the warmongers. While he was speaking, a man in the third row got up;
he walked up to the podium, drew a gun, and shot both the
speaker and the professor.

Again, panic and confusion; again, the audience scrambling for
the exits; and again:

"Wait! Wait a moment!"

The audience turned to the podium, and there stood the two
men who had fired the shots, as well as the professor—all three
of them smiling; the second gunman then explained once more
that the incident had been just an act to give the public a
dramatic, and therefore didactic, demonstration of the savage and
treacherous methods of the warmongers. While he was speaking,
a man in the sixth row stood up; he walked up to the podium,
drew a gun, then shot the speaker, the fellow who had previously
staged the act, and the professor. This time the panic and confusion weren't as great; people walked toward the exits but in no
great hurry; and when the man shouted for them to wait, they
returned calmly to their seats. The third gunman then explained
that the whole thing had been just an act, etc. And at that point a
man in the fifth row stood up.

There was a succession of such acts, with the shooting followed by an explanation. Except that now the people heading for
the exits were in fact leaving; it was getting late and the whole
thing had become an utter bore. Finally, there was only one
person in the auditorium, although by then there was quite a
crowd on the stage itself—the professor and all the fake gunmen.
The last of these gunmen was explaining that the whole thing
had been nothing but an act, etc., when the lone member of the
audience rose from his seat in the twentieth row; he walked up
to the podium, and, taking a machine gun from under his

raincoat, he opened fire on the current speaker and everyone else around him. When he was finished, he left.

There was no one else in the auditorium; therefore, nobody went up to the stage to find out whether or not the men were dying. As it turned out, they did die—which happened in minutes or years.

BURNING ANGELS

It happens at any time of the day or night, even in the course of a meal, or during a party. Suddenly, Munhoz becomes pale and distressed. The film, I've completely forgotten about it, he mumbles, and runs to the small room that he uses as a photographer's studio. Everybody knows, however, that he's not going there to develop films: it is an open secret.

As soon as he enters the studio, he lights a candle. In the dimly lit environment, his face, which has absolutely ordinary features, acquires a phantasmagoric expression: a prelude to what is about to happen.

Motionless, his mouth partly open, Munhoz waits. If after four or five minutes nothing of what is supposed to happen happens, he makes a sound with his lips, the kind of sound that others would make to attract doves. Then, at that moment, from the cracks in the wall and from amid the piles of cardboard boxes that fill the shelves, comes something like a crackling sound, soon followed by a faint rustling and buzzing—and what has Munhoz got now?

Angels begin to flutter around the candle. Diminutive, they are: not more than two centimeters tall. It would be really difficult to fit them into the same category of the celestial creatures who, to the right and to the left of God, intone hosannas. It is well known, however, that when it comes to angels, there's room for a great diversity in appearance; besides, their tiny white cotton robes and the lyres they carry affixed to their backs are unmistakable. Angels, yes. Miniature angels, but angels nevertheless.

The light attracts them in the same way that beautiful women attract certain men. They describe circles, which grow increasingly smaller, around the flame of the candle. From a corner Munhoz watches them surreptitiously. With apprehension: He foresees what is going to happen.

The angels draw closer and closer to the flame; they are now just millimeters away. Then suddenly the robe of one of the angels catches fire, and, floundering, he falls to the floor, a horrible sight to behold. But it's a short-lived agony: A small noise, something like a muffled shriek, is heard, and presto, it's all over with that angel. The same happens to another angel, and soon to another, and thus, in a short while, eight or nine angels are exterminated by fire.

Munhoz does nothing to prevent the carnage. On the contrary, he derives pleasure from what he sees. He smiles, rubs his hands, and doesn't leave until the last little angel has been reduced to ashes. By then there is a lack of oxygen in the small room: The flame flickers, already on the point of becoming extinguished, and Munhoz himself feels asphyxiated.

He leaves his room to face the reproachful eyes of the members of his family. Munhoz is aware of what they say about him: That he is wicked, that he takes the trouble of dressing beetles like angels, only to immolate them in the fire.

Munhoz doesn't accept such accusations. The winged beings go to their death because they want to; he doesn't prevail upon them to do so. Besides, these creatures aren't the charming insects know as beetles. They are indeed angels.

FREE TOPICS

BECAUSE OF THE TIME LIMIT, I'LL BE BRIEF. THE PURPOSE OF MY presentation is to relate the results of a survey conducted in one of our suburbs, Vila Armênia, to find out about consumer practices among the lower classes. Since time is short, I'll abstain from dealing with the question of methodology and go straight to the conclusions.

The first slide, please. There you see, ladies and gentlemen, the universe that we've researched: a thousand and one hundred people, sixty-two percent of whom are female.... And you can see the other details for yourselves, I'm not going to examine them because I'm pressed for time.... The second slide, please. There you can see the distribution by age group.... Most of the population consists of children and young adults.... The next one, please, quick, because we haven't got much time left, the chairman of the board is already signaling to me.... Here's a chart showing family income.... The income of some of these people is less than the minimum wage.... Next. This slide shows consumer practices.... It refers to the tobacco question.... As you can see, about one third of the cross-section smokes. You can well imagine which brands of cigarette are favored. Next. This one here refers to the mass media. Notice that the majority prefers radio, followed by television.... Next. There you have their eating habits.... It's a complex chart, so I won't be able to go into it.... How much time have I got left Mr. Chairman...? Two minutes. Well, let's press on. Next! This slide isn't very important, let's go to the next one.... This one refers to entertainment.... In this suburb in particular, the townspeople have a big barn dance that's very popular. My own wife did research on it. Next. Well, this slide is only to show you the team that conducted the research on this barn dance of theirs. The one standing over there with a smile, that's me, of course. That's my wife by my side. The young man with the mustache is Chico, one of the local residents who helped us a lot in the course of our work.... Next. That's a shot of the barn dance: there's my wife dancing with Chico.... Next. There's my wife arriving at a motel together with Chico. The motel, it was later discovered, was my wife's own choice. This Chico had never until then set foot in a motel. Next. I took this picture through the window, see.... the two of them lying there.... Observe the lascivious expression on her face, the glitter in her eyes.... Observe that salacious smile.... She's spreading for him.... And he's drooling over her.... Just look at him, see if he's not.... Look carefully, because time is running out. Time's up, isn't that right, Mr. Chairman? It is. That's it, then; time's up. That's for sure. Lights on, please. Please, lights on.

THE PASSWORD

An old corporal is returning to his army camp late at night. His figure is barely discernible in the faint moonlight that bathes the stretch of prairie land; it's not surprising, therefore, that the sentry, weapon in hand, should order him to halt and not make another move. The corporal stops, annoyed (he can barely stand on his feet, and is eager to lie down), but he is not alarmed. The soldier draws near.

"The password."

Password? What's going on? Password? He tries to remember. His mind—befogged with drink, for he had been imbibing all evening—isn't of much help, but he somehow manages to remember: Yes, there's something. Some new rule: Nobody can enter the camp without giving the password. As a matter of fact, he himself relayed this rule to the rank and file. But the thing is, the password now escapes him. It's a word ... or a phrase ... It's no good, he can't remember it. The soldier persists: The password, give me the password. Be patient, will

you? mutters the corporal, I'm trying to remember. He hazards
some humor.

"I'm old, son. Old people forget things, especially things like
passwords."

Impassive, the soldier looks fixedly at him. Obviously, he
doesn't care for humor—or for explanations. He wants the password. The soldier's stubbornness irritates the corporal. Dammit,
don't you recognize me? he asks. I do, replies the soldier, I
recognize you perfectly well, but I want the password; without
the password nobody enters the camp. But I can't recall it, says
the corporal, let me in, will you? I'm sleepy, who's going to know
I didn't give you the password? The soldier makes no reply.
Motionless, weapon in hand, he waits.

The corporal tries to remember. Is it a word, or is it a phrase?
In his effort to remember, he closes his eyes, his face screwed up
in a painful grimace. Phrase or word? It must be a word. But
there are so many words, so very many. Even a humble, almost
illiterate man like him must know millions of words. From the
dusty corners in the dark cellar of his memory, the words are
now watching him. Then he starts searching for one, groping
about in the dark with difficulty, trying to fit the sounds of every
word that occurs to him into the ill-defined mold he has in his
head. Naturally, he starts with the most imposing words. Is it
pátria, fatherland? No, it can't be *pátria*, *pátria* is a word of the
feminine gender, and he thinks (but perhaps this is just a macho
hangup) that no word of the feminine gender would be used as a
password. Is it *duty*? Is it *heroism*? Or is it a combination of two
words, like *duty discharged*? It occurs to him that he may have
jotted down the password on a scrap of paper, which he then put
into his pocket. He often does this: He writes things down in
order not to forget them. Sometimes he forgets where he wrote
them down. But in the case of the password, it's possible that he
has it on him. Thrusting his hands into his pockets, he empties

them out: money, identification papers, medical prescriptions, a letter from his daughter, a pack of cigarettes. Each piece is examined, for the password might have been jotted down on the pack of cigarettes, for instance, or on the back of a receipt. And indeed, there is something written on the back of a receipt; something he can't read in the semi-darkness. Have you got a lantern? he asks the soldier. The youth says he hasn't. You're on duty as sentry and you haven't got a lantern? The corporal finds it peculiar. I haven't got one, repeats the soldier. The corporal searches for traces of irritation or mockery in the soldier's tone of voice; there aren't any. The tone is neutral; there's no reason for the corporal to suspect harassment. The corporal squats down, lays the receipt on the ground, strikes a match, and tries to read what's on it. A complicated operation, for he can barely coordinate his gestures; besides, the wind keeps extinguishing the flame. But there is something written down, and finally he manages to read: *horse*.

Horse. Could this be the password? It's impossible for him to remember. If this is the password, wouldn't he be overcome by sudden jubilation, by that kind of joy that strikes scientists upon making a new discovery, or gamblers upon hitting the jackpot? Perhaps. Perhaps his age and all he has been through in life have cast a damper over such raptures of joy. *Horse*, even if it doesn't kindle enthusiasm, could well be the password. Could it, really? Is it possible that the lieutenant—the man responsible for passwords—could have chosen such a word? A word not entirely ridiculous, of course, but somewhat silly. Why horse? There are no horses in the camp. There are farms in the area—but would this fact be sufficient reason for the lieutenant to have chosen the word *horse* as a password?

On the other hand, if it is not the password, why in the world did he write it down? He usually jots down things that he is supposed to buy to take home, things that his wife wants him to get; but was there a moment when he considered buying a horse? (And where would he find the money to buy one?) Was there a moment when his wife asked him for a horse? Could the word stand for something else, say, a tip on the illegal animal numbers game? No, he has never gambled on the animal numbers games. He wouldn't even know how to go about it. He's not a gambler at all. He's an honest corporal who sometimes drinks too much—but then, who doesn't? Is there anyone who doesn't get stewed to the gills every once in a while, especially if he happens to have a daughter in poor health, and a mentally retarded son? Horse. A mystery, this horse.

He looks at the soldier who, impassive, continues to look fixedly at him. The corporal could test out the word. He could say *horse* in the casual tone of someone speaking to himself. If this is the password, then everything will be fine; the sentry will let him enter the camp; if it is not, it could be interpreted as a drunkard's muttering. Before saying the word, however, the corporal decides to see what else is on the list; the next word is *orange*, yes, he promised to take some oranges home, his wife wanted to use them in a dessert. Such a good, talented woman.... Therefore, orange is not the password; or is it? Could it be that besides alluding to one of the ingredients in the dessert, it is also the password? Rather unlikely.

The third and fourth words are absolutely illegible. He strikes one match after the other, trying to read his own scrawl, but he can't; his handwriting has always been atrocious. During his few years of schooling, his teachers kept warning him: You'll have to improve your handwriting, or one day you'll get into hot water. And that's precisely where he finds himself now—in hot water. Because quite possibly, the password is there, lost in this illegible scrawl of his.

The light of the match goes out. It's his last one, too. With difficulty the corporal stands up, looks at the soldier—and he is overcome by a sudden fit of anger. No, he doesn't remember the password. And so what? He's not obliged to remember every single thing he is told, there's enough nonsense in his head already. He has forgotten it, that's it. He feels like sending the soldier packing; but he can't, he's not in a position to do something like that. Instead, he tries reasoning, and argues that in fact, he knows the password, that he has it stored somewhere inside him, that it's only a matter of pulling it out of the bottom of the well of memory. All he needs is time. And perhaps a hint. Yes: A hint would help.

I'm not giving you any hint, says the soldier in the same neutral tone as before; every man has to remember the password unaided. Oh, yeah? says the corporal with indignation. Every man for himself, is that so? Unaided, repeats the soldier.

"And what if you were on the battlefield? What if you lay wounded on the battlefield? Would it still be every man for himself? Or would you at that moment ask for help?"

The soldier makes no reply. Those are his tactics, concludes the corporal—not to make a reply, not to get involved. The password. That's all he cares about. The password? He'll get the password. The corporal will utter every single word he remembers. Every one of them. Beginning with the most important ones in the life of a warrior.

"Cannon! Is cannon the password? Hmm? Is it cannon? Is it rifle? Is it bayonet? Is it mortar? Is it ammunition? Is it howitzer? Is it shrapnel? Is it tank? Is it flask? Is it haversack? Is it binoculars?"

The soldier, impassive. But the corporal continues; after the words related to the army camp, others from the civilian life come to his mind—house, wardrobe, bed, patriot, bathroom, store; then, words at random—moon, star, sea, brook; next, names of plants, of animals (including *horse*); finally, swear words: finally, one single swear word:

"Shit, shit, shit, shit," he repeats in a monotone. "Shit, shit."
Panting, the corporal falls silent. He stands glowering at the
soldier; he's angry, really angry.

But he controls himself. *Take it easy, you old corporal, take it
easy, you idiot. Don't lose your head. Think it over, put on your
thinking cap.* Yep, it will take cleverness. It will take some
bargaining, I'll have to win this guy over, after all, he's merely
carrying out his duty. And what's more (and at this thought the
corporal even becomes softhearted), there was a time when he,
too, was a young recruit who took pride in being on guard at the
gates of the barracks.

No, he has no reason to quarrel with the soldier; they are
brothers in arms—the corporal the older brother, the soldier, his
kid brother. It falls on the older brother to be tolerant and
understanding, to give in when there's an impasse.

"Well? What do you say?"

"I say that I want the password," replies the soldier in a firm
voice.

"Yeah, sure, the password. But before I—"

"The password!"

The soldier cocks his rifle. The corporal takes a deep breath.
The moment has come, at last. It would have to come one day,
and now it has come. It is something that the corporal has always
feared: How am I going to behave? Because, even though he is a
military man, he has always been a peaceable person, he has never
quarreled with anybody. And what is more, he has never been in
a narrow-escape situation, he has never been seriously ill, he has
never undergone surgery. And now the moment has come. Suddenly, without forewarning. Triggered by something stupid: first
the drinking spree, then this password thing. He would have
expected something more solemn, more spectacular. Sometimes
he would think of a war, and in his imagination he would see
himself collapse, wounded, on the battlefield. But we're in Brazil:

we're peace-loving, not warmongering people. Sometimes we have to make threats, take security measures, but deep down everybody knows they aren't for real. Everybody? No. This little soldier here doesn't know. And there's no time to teach him now, it's too late. There's no time to say, look here, buddy, forget it, nothing of this is to be taken seriously.

Nevertheless, the whole thing is the staging of an act. An act in which the corporal has to play his role. Reluctantly, for he's tired and sleepy, but there's no other way. The youth must be taught a lesson. So, with a sigh, the corporal smiles—but there's nothing ironic in his smile, he's sure there isn't; nothing challenging, either—and he steps forward. The soldier, motionless, looks at him. Six footsteps, ten footsteps, twenty footsteps, and now the corporal's back is already turned to the soldier—and at this moment, so unbearable is his anxiety, and so violent the contraction of the muscles in his neck, in his back, even in his scalp, that he—but this takes but a fraction of a second—stops short. The moment he stops, though, a dead calm invades him; it's as if he were floating on a huge lake of tepid waters. And as in a dream, he resumes walking. He's not going to shoot me in the back, the corporal is thinking with diffident joy. He won't do such a thing, nobody would.

But then he stops again: And he turns around; he opens his arms—and there's a blast, and he falls to the ground, the smile frozen on his face at the precise moment when he was about to utter—and why was it that he just couldn't recall it before?—the password, the real password, so obvious it was, this password, which he had on the tip of his tongue, and which was, yes, precisely that: *a dead shot.*

THE EMISSARY

ON SATURDAYS I WOULD VISIT HIM IN THE HOSPITAL. EVERY time I saw him, I thought he looked worse. But to him I would say: You're looking good, Pedro. To which he would reply with an impatient—and yet grateful, undoubtedly grateful—gesture.

I would sit down and give him the usual small bag of apples (he would thank me; he wouldn't eat them, though; could this perhaps explain why he was getting worse?). Then he would chat for a while—about the weather, about the news in the papers—but I was well aware that he wasn't interested in any of it. I always sensed that he was eager to go straight to the point. But even so, we—he or I, or both of us—would prolong the small talk. Anyhow, it fell on me to give the cue.

"I saw Teresa yesterday." The tone of voice was, of course, nonchalant.

He: "Did you?" trying, of course, to show little interest. I would wait for a while before continuing with a carefully thought out statement.

"She struck me as being rather down and out."

"What makes you think so?" he would say, barely containing his anxiety. "She was shabbily dressed," I would reply—and from then on the conversation would proceed in a crescendo. I: She struck me as being rather ill. He: Poor thing—a remark made with some pleasure. I: She's been evicted from her apartment. He: Poor thing—a remark made with a small smile—poor thing! I: She's been hitting the bottle. He: Ah! I: She now walks with a gimp. He: The poor bitch! I: Her women friends have been shunning her. He: You don't say! I: It's true, Pedro. She's really gone to seed. He: Oh God.

He would throw his hands up and let himself collapse on the pillow, where he would lie panting, eyes closed, nostrils quivering. In a state of bliss, obviously. In seventh heaven.

I would wait in silence. Soon he would open one eye: Tell me more, he would ask.

I would look at my watch: I can't Pedro, I must be going now.

He would beg: For the love of God. But I would remain adamant in my refusal to tell him more. I had a feeling that it was his curiosity that kept him alive. And I wanted him alive.

Because Teresa always got a kick out of it whenever I said: I went to see Pedro in the hospital.

Tell me all about it, she would then say with a small smile, do tell me what you've seen.

I always told her. Which gave Teresa great pleasure. And I was not one to deny Teresa a pleasure.

THE CANDIDATE

WE ARE A GROUP OF ABOUT THIRTY ENTREPRENEURS WORKING IN all lines of business. We do not, however, constitute an association; what brings us together are our common interests—not always brought up at our dinner parties, as well as the bonds of friendship among some of us—the latter always extolled on the occasion of drinking a toast. Menezes is our leader. Neither the oldest nor the richest among us, he is, however, a man of vision, and for this reason his opinions are always respected. Therefore, when he said that we needed a representative in the City Council, we agreed right away. Since the elections would be held five months from then, we would have to set things in motion without delay. Menezes himself volunteered to search for a candidate. His incredible efficiency was again in evidence: At the following dinner party he was already announcing that he had found the ideal person for our purposes.

"Young, charming, elegant, articulate, smart as a tack. He rose from nothing. Do you really know what nothing is?" He gave us a challenging look. "Many of you claim that you rose from nothing, but that's not so. Your nothing and his nothing are not the same. All of you had something, some education, a relative with clout, some money you inherited, even if it was a mere pittance. Whereas he—you can't even imagine the kind of life he had. The father, a drunk. The mother, in poor health. They lived in a shack. Often, there was nothing to eat. Very early in life he was forced to earn a living. He attended school in the evenings. He soon distinguished himself in student politics and in soccer, both of which, he told me, gave him his remarkable sense of timing. He graduated in law. He married the daughter of a merchant, a wealthy man who unfortunately lost everything in a series of unsuccessful business ventures. But this fact is of no consequence to him because, he told me, he wants to make it on his own. For this reason he is willing to have a go at anything. What do you say, gentlemen? Is he eligible?"

We had to agree: He was eligible. Then, excusing himself, Menezes left the hall and soon returned accompanied by a man still young and—just as he had told us—charming and elegant. That he was articulate and clever became apparent as soon as he started to speak. Everybody was thrilled; but I, and I don't know exactly why, hesitated. It was a slight hesitation, but hesitation nonetheless. Caused perhaps, by a certain expression that I saw, or thought that I saw at one moment on the closely shaved face of our candidate. At one moment, on that face, I detected, or thought that I detected (perhaps because of a certain innate distrust in my nature, a trait that I have never succeeded in shaking off, not withstanding the great harm it has already caused me), an expression of a certain melancholy; at one moment his look became vacant, the corners of his mouth drooped, and all of a sudden he looked much older than his twenty-seven years. But this melancholy, whether real or imagined, vanished immediately, and soon he was laughing and greeting one and all with handshakes and hugs.

Menezes was right. The election campaign turned out to be expensive, but the young man got an impressive number of votes. Quite pleased, we decided to have a dinner party in his honor. On the night of the dinner we were all gathered at the club, still jubilant over our victory—but he was late. Eight o'clock, eight-thirty, nine, nine-thirty—and still no sign of him. Some of us were already annoyed: The fellow is already getting up on his high horse was a comment I heard in various groups. We were thinking of starting dinner without him (this would teach him a lesson, too), when an employee of the club came to say that there was a phone call for Menezes. Menezes went to the phone and returned soon, looking pale. He drew me aside.

"It was his wife. She asked us to hurry there. He's in his study, with a gun on his head, threatening to kill himself."

We—Menezes and I—went there in a taxi. The woman was waiting at the door. Tearful, she told us that her husband sometimes had these bouts of depression, but they were rare, and nobody knew about them because he never mentioned the matter; this time, however, things had gone too far, and frightened, she had decided to call on us for help. She showed us into his study. And indeed, there was our alderman with the gun barrel against his head. What struck me right away was the expression of deep melancholy on his face: the vacant look, the drooping corners of his mouth.

Placing himself in front of the young man, Menezes fixed his eyes on him.

"How much?" Menezes asked in a firm voice.

Our alderman looked at Menezes as if he hadn't understood. "Come on," Menezes insisted, "we've got no time to waste; tell me straight out, how much do you want not to kill yourself?"

Slowly, a smile began to open the young man's face.

"A lot," he said.

"We'll talk about it later," Menezes said. Then, taking the gun from the young man's hand, he put it into his pocket. "Let's go now, we're already late for dinner."

We got into the taxi; I sat on the front seat next to the cabbie. Menezes and the alderman, together on the backseat, were engaged in a lively conversation. I was now convinced that this aldermanship was going to cost us a lot of money; but I was also convinced that it was money well invested.

GENERAL DELIVERY

ONE DAY I GOT OUT OF BED, WASHED MY FACE, COMBED MY hair, got dressed, drank coffee, and went to the house of the widow Paulina, a neighbor of ours.

The widow Paulina was an elderly lady, very friendly. For this reason, and also because she was an invalid (she moved about in a wheelchair), I was always rendering her a small service, such as mowing the lawn in her garden, walking her dog, Pinoquio, and mailing her letters at the post office.

There were always heaps of letters. The widow Paulina subscribed to a publication that listed pen pals all over the world. Thus, she would write to countries as distant as Sri Lanka, Japan, Tunisia. Letters and more letters; a good part of her modest income was spent on postage. With almost negative results; only occasionally did she receive a reply. But this fact didn't discourage her; on the contrary, she stepped up her letter-writing. By writing letters, according to her, she remained faithful to the memory of her husband, a humanitarian doctor who, to his dying day, had dreamed of a united world. To his widow he had bequeathed a message of love. And little else: a few old books, an ancient car, which she sold, and a modest nest egg. He hadn't owned much because his patients, who were poor, couldn't afford to pay him—a fact that the widow always recalled with emotion. My father had been one of his patients. So, there was also a component of gratitude in my lending assistance to the old lady.

Well, I dropped in on the widow Paulina. She was waiting for me in the garden, smiling as usual. She asked how I was doing in school, and gave me a slice of the cake that she had baked herself. Then she handed me a letter. Just one? I found it strange. Yes, just one, she replied, giving me a level look. Taking the letter and the money, I said good-bye and left.

As usual, I headed for the park. I threw away the piece of cake—it tasted awful—sat down on a bench, and, as I always did, I opened the letter. By and large, I got a kick out of reading her letters.

On that day, however, I was in for a surprise.

The letter was written to me. The envelope itself was addressed to somebody in the United States, but the letter, the letter itself, started with a *Dear Chico*. Chico, that's me. It's my nickname.

And the widow wrote on: *I would never expect this kind of thing from you, Chico. You, of whom I've been so fond.*

The fact is that she had found me out. She knew that I didn't mail her letters, that I pocketed the money for the stamps. The new post office master, who happened to be a relative of hers, told her that I never set foot in the post office. And the widow concluded by saying: *To think that I trusted you. To think that I handed you the money taken from my dwindling savings when instead I could have invested it. I could have exchanged it into dollars, Chico.*

Crumbling the letter, I threw it away. *Dollars!* I would keep this in mind until it was time for me to make my first investments.

IN THE SUBMARINE RESTAURANT

JERÔNIMO RINGS ME UP. I HAVE SOME GREAT NEWS, HE SAYS, the excitement in his voice sounding strange in a man who is normally reserved. Great news, he repeats, adding that he can't tell me about it over the phone. He suggests that we meet for lunch: the two of us, and also Hélio and Sadi. Where? I ask, rather uneasy. At the Submarine Restaurant, he replies. I argue that it's way out; besides, it's not the best time of the year to go to the Submarine Restaurant; not in this cold, rainy weather. That's precisely why we're going there, says Jerônimo, I don't want anybody to see us. As a matter of fact, I've already phoned and reserved the entire restaurant just for us.

I ended up accepting the invitation. What else? Jerônimo is well known for his tenacity, for his iron will. He lets nothing stand in his way, that's what everybody says about him.

I drive to the place where the Submarine Restaurant is located. On the highway, I'm overtaken by Hélio, who looks at me with an inquiring expression. It seems that he, too, doesn't know what is going on.

Upon arriving at the beach, I leave my car in the parking lot. The cars of the others are already parked there. As usual, I'm the last one to arrive.

I walk along the ancient wharf, at the end of which the restaurant was built. Entering the lobby, I greet the circumspect manager, then climb down the winding staircase. The restaurant proper is below sea level. Through its windows, or rather scuttles, diners can watch the marine fauna of the area.

Jerônimo and the others are seated at a table in a corner. Greeting them, I take a seat. They are engaged in small talk. But it's obvious that Jerônimo is radiant.

A loudspeaker placed right above our heads squeaks, then emits a shrill sound. "Hello!" says a man's voice. "Hello, hello. Testing, testing. One, two, three. One, two, three. Testing, testing."

A pause, then the voice goes on.

"Gentlemen, welcome to the Submarine Restaurant, the only one of its kind in Brazil. The management would like you to make yourselves at home. While you savor our delectable dishes, we'll give you some information about the marine creatures surrounding us. We'll return in a few moments. Thank you for now."

Hélio, who had never been to the place, is amazed. Wonderfully well appointed, isn't it? he says. What an ingenious idea!

"Attention," it's the loudspeaker again. "Gentlemen, your attention, please. There's an octopus approaching us from the south. The octopus, gentlemen, is not a fish, it's a mollusk. I repeat: a mollusk. And here comes our hero!"

It is, in fact, a small octopus. Slowly, it passes across our scuttle and disappears. Fantastic, cries out the enthusiastic Hélio. This place here is fantastic, Jerônimo! Jerônimo says nothing; he merely smiles.

The loudspeaker again:

"Attention! What we see now is a dogfish. It's a close relative of the shark, the killer of the seas."

Swiftly, the dogfish swims away.

The waiter comes with a huge platter. I took the liberty of ordering this for all of us, Jerônimo explains. You're going to like it. It's snook. Super. Really super.

I don't like fish, says Sadi, I'd rather have shrimp. His voice is tinged with huffiness; but Jerônimo is already asking the waiter to get his shrimp. Certainly, sir, says the waiter, who then goes away.

Jerônimo raises his glass: To us, he says. We drink and afterward silence falls upon us, a silence that strikes me (but then, I'm rather paranoid) as oppressive. I lean toward him.

"Well, let's hear what you have to say to us."

Jerônimo takes another sip of wine. Good, this wine, he remarks. He wipes his lips with the napkin, looks at us—always smiling—and announces: "The man's finished. He'll be kicked out next week. And I'll get the post, it's in the bag! Can I count on you?"

But you're a genius, Hélio cries out. A real genius, I agree. Only Sadi says nothing. He's looking through the scuttle: There's a school of fish out there. The loudspeaker doesn't tell us their name, but I'll bet they are robalo, also known as snook. They stare at Sadi with their inexpressive eyes.

PEACE AND WAR

BEING LATE FOR THE WAR, I HAD TO TAKE A TAXI. MUCH TO my annoyance: with the recent increase in the taxi fares, this expense, unforeseen and ill timed, was a hole in my budget. However, I did make it, and was able to clock in just in the nick of time, thus averting further hassles. There was a long line of people waiting to get to the time clock: I wasn't the only latecomer. Walter, my partner in the trench, was there, too, muttering: Like me, he had been forced to take a taxi. We were neighbors and we had joined the war roughly at the same time. Every second Thursday of each month we would take a bus at an intersection of our street in order to take part in the war activities.

I'm sick and tired of the whole shebang, said Walter. Me, too, I replied. Sighing, we clocked in and headed for the quartermaster's depot, where the locker room was temporarily (but this had been so for over fifteen years) located. Aren't you late today? asked the youth in charge of the locker room. We made no reply. He handed us the keys to our lockers. Quickly, we changed out of our clothes and into our old fatigues; then, grabbing the rifles and the ammnunition (twenty cartridges), we headed for the line of battle.

The setting for the armed conflict was a stretch of prairie land on the outskirts of the city. The battlefield was surrounded by a barbed-wire fence with signs saying WAR, KEEP OUT. An unnecessary warning: hardly anybody went there, to that site of bucolic granges and small farms.

We, the soldiers, occupied a trench roughly two kilometers long. The enemy, whom we had never seen, were about a kilometer away from us, and they, too, were entrenched. The terrain between the two trenches was littered with debris: wrecked tanks and other destroyed armored vehicles lay jumbled together with skeletons of horses—reminders of a time when the fighting had been fierce. But now the conflict had reached a stable phase—of upkeep, in the words of our commander. Battles were no longer fought. But even so, our orders were not to leave the trench. Which posed a problem to me: My youngest son wanted me to get him an empty shell fired from a howitzer, but there was no way I could get one. My kid kept pestering me about it, but there was nothing I could do.

We—Walter and I—climbed down to the trench. The place wasn't totally lacking in amenities. It was furnished with tables, chairs, a small stove, kitchen utensils, not to mention a sound system and a portable television set. I suggested that Walter and I play a game of cards. Later, he said. With a wrinkled forehead and an air of dissatisfaction, he was examining his rifle: This fucking thing doesn't work anymore, he stated. But after all, I said, it is more than fifteen years old, it has seen better days. Then I offered him my own weapon: I had no intention of ever firing a shot. Just then we heard a detonation and a bullet came hissing over our heads. That was a near miss, I said. The idiots, muttered Walter, one of these days they'll end up hurting some-

one. Grabbing my weapon, he rose to his feet and fired two shots
in the air. That's a warning to you, he shouted, and sat down
again. A manservant appeared holding a cordless telephone:
Your wife, Senhor Walter. What the devil, Walter cried out, not
even here will this woman leave me in peace. He took the phone.
"Hello! Yes, that's me. I'm fine. Of course I'm fine. No,
nothing has happened to me, I've already told you, I'm fine. I
know you get nervous, but there's no reason why you should.
Everything's okay, I'm well sheltered, it isn't raining. Did you
hear me? Everything's okay. There's no need to apologize. I
understand. A kiss."

What an utter bore, this woman, he said, handing the phone
back to the manservant. I said nothing. I, too, had a problem
with my wife, but of a different nature. She didn't believe that
we were at war. Her suspicion was that I was spending the day
in a motel with someone else. I would like to explain to her the
nature of this war, but in fact, I myself didn't know. Nobody
knew. It was a very confusing thing; so much so that a committee had been set put to study the situation of the conflict. The
chairman of this committee would sometimes visit us, and then
he would complain about the car he had been given to go on
these inspection trips: a jalopy, according to him. It was, in fact, a
very old car. To practice economy, his superiors wouldn't change
it for a newer model.

The morning went by serenely; somebody from our side fired
a shot, somebody from the other side fired back, and that was all.
At noon we were served lunch. A green salad, roast beef, rice
prepared in the Greek style; for dessert, an insipid pudding. This
is really going downhill, Walter grumbled. The waiter asked him
if he thought this place was a restaurant or what. Walter made
no reply.

We lay down for a nap and slept peacefully. When we woke
up, night was falling. I think I'll go home now, I said to Walter.

He couldn't leave with me: He was on duty that night. I went to the locker room and changed. How was the war? the smart-alecky youth asked me. Good, I replied, really good. I dropped by the administration office, got my paycheck from a sour-looking employee, and signed all three copies of the receipt. And I arrived at the bus stop just in the nick of time.

At home, my wife, dressed in a leotard, was waiting for me. I'm ready, she said dryly. I went to the bedroom to get my sweatshirt. We went to the fitness gym and mounted the exercise bicycles. Where exactly were we? I asked. You never seem to know, she answered in a reproachful tone. Picking up the map, she studied it for a moment, then said: "Bisceglie, on the Adriatic coast."

We started pedaling vigorously; when we stopped two hours later, we were approaching Molfeta, still on the Adriatic coast. We figure it will take us a year to complete the circuit of Italy. Then, we'll wait and see. I dislike making long-term plans; because of the war, of course, but mostly because the unknown element of the future is for me a source of constant excitement.

THE BLANK

At the age of ten he decides to keep a diary—and from then on there won't be a day when he doesn't record something—an event, a thought, a daydream. The years go by, the notebooks pile up. At the age of fifty, the man, driven by some obscure motive, decides to review, not his life, but his diaries. It is something he never did before. So, he reads on, at times with a smile; at times with tears in his eyes; at times enraptured; at times bored. Suddenly, he realizes that there is no entry at all for one particular day; it is the only day when he wrote nothing, as he verifies by leafing through the rest of this notebook and of all the others that followed it. Why, he wonders. Why is this particular day missing? At first the most obvious reason occurs to him—a leaf torn from the notebook. But no: The same page on which the entry for that particular day should have been also contains the entries for both the preceding and the following days. Brief notes as a matter of fact, like all the others. He is, therefore, facing an inexplicable fact: an unrecorded day.

Why? Because of a trip? No. Even when he went on a trip, he always took the diary with him. An illness? Again, no. Even when ill (and he was never seriously ill), he never failed to record something. What was initially intriguing has now become a torment: The man doesn't want merely to find out, he *has* to. The mystery tortures him, he has lost his appetite, he can't concentrate on his work. His wife and friends ask him what is wrong: They've never seen him like this. But there's no one he can tell anything because he feels that nobody would understand him.

He is determined to clear up this mystery. It won't be easy. At the time when that particular entry should have been made, he was living alone. Newly graduated from college he was still jobless. And it wasn't until months later that he found a girlfriend. So, there were no connecting elements, nobody he could ask. To whom should he turn for help? After mulling over the matter, he goes to a fortune-teller who, rather surprised, says there's nothing he can do. He specializes in predicting the future, not in disclosing the past. He suggests that the man go to a hypnotist. The man tries hypnosis, but without success; whenever he is about to fall into a trance, he is frightened, and is again on his guard. Noticing the man's great anxiety, the hypnotist advises him to see a psychologist. The man goes to a psychologist, who listens to him attentively for forty minutes; at the end of the session, the psychologist shakes his head and looks at the man sympathetically. Yes, he says, the memory of that day must be in your subconscious, buried somewhere deep down, but I don't see how I can retrieve it. He gives the man some hope, though: It's possible that it will surface unexpectedly, like the corpse of a drowned man.

"Maybe during a dream. Pay attention to your dreams."

The man begins to sleep with pencil and notebook at hand. Should a dream bring him the recollection he has been yearning to remember, he wants to write it down immediately, before he forgets it again. Then one night, he does in fact remember; he remembers everything; with a trembling hand he writes down in the notebook what he has remembered, then, exhausted but pleased, he falls asleep. In the morning he discovers that the pages in the notebook are blank. The act of writing something down was also a dream.

Now the man is convinced that something serious must have happened. He goes to the morgue of a major morning newspaper and ask the person in charge for a copy of the newspaper published on that fateful day. The attendant brings him the requested newspaper and the man leafs through it impatiently. Then, in the crime section, he finds what he has been searching for. A loner was murdered, and the police had no clues.

The man doesn't feel well. He goes to the men's room and washes his face. Then he raises his head, and in the mirror he sees the smiling face of his victim.

MANY MANY METERS ABOVE
GOOD AND EVIL

AT THE END OF THE STREET THERE WAS AN EMPTY LOT, AND at the back of this lot stood the house in ruins where Lúcia and I used to play. Everybody said that the house was haunted, that ghosts were often seen there. But Lúcia and I weren't afraid. We feared nothing. We were both ten years old then, an age when children are usually afraid of ghosts; we, however, were afraid of nothing—until one afternoon, as we were about to enter the house, we heard muffled moanings coming from inside. A moment later I was already far away from the house, with my hair standing on end and my heart pounding fiercely. Lúcia didn't run away. Come back here, she shouted, this is no ghost, it's a person.

Warily, I approached the house. The two of us went in. We waited until our eyes got adjusted to the darkness. Look, over there, whispered Lúcia.

I looked and saw an old man—the oldest and most shriveled old man I had ever seen. He was lying behind a heap of bricks, all huddled up inside his tattered clothes.

Lúcia squatted down by his side and remained looking at him. I would rather have fled, but she seemed fascinated by that old ragamuffin who looked ill—and who stank something fierce. "Are you feeling ill?" she asked, a question that struck me as obviously unnecessary; the old man was ill, desperately ill. He didn't even make a reply; he moaned and moaned. Lúcia put her hand on his forehead. "Does he have a temperature?" I asked. "I don't think so," she said, "it feels ice cold, poor little fellow."

(Poor little fellow. That's how she would refer to the old man from then on: *poor little fellow*. The poor little fellow is hungry. The poor little fellow is cold. We never found out his name.)

Lúcia rose to her feet, her mind made up: We're going to bring him food. Food, clothes, and a blanket.

I wasn't in complete agreement with her. Yes, I thought that the old man was possibly starving and freezing; it was winter, and winters in Rio Grande do Sul can be severe; however, to take steps to supply the old man with the basic necessities and look after him was a whole new ball game. We had better notify someone, a neighbor, the police.

"Lúcia, maybe we should . . ."

But she wasn't even listening. Already acting on her decision, she ran to her house and was back in a jiffy with bread, a chicken leg, apples; then she began to press food on the old man. A well-intentioned but useless try. Whimpering, the creature kept shaking his head. Lúcia stood staring at him, her forehead creased. I know, she finally said. He can't eat because he's got no teeth.

Again, she ran home and returned with her baby sister's feeding bottle, which she had filled with milk. She inserted the nipple into the old man's mouth and he began to suck it ravenously. The problem is solved, she said, pleased.

Was the problem solved? I didn't think so. How were we going to look after the old man, there, in that house in ruins?

And without anybody knowing? (For Lúcia had sworn me to secrecy: Don't tell anyone, not even your brothers.)

She entrusted me with the task of arranging for clothes and blankets. In the attic of my house there was a chest containing the belongings of my dead grandfather, and that's where I got hold of those items. And I even took a mattress to the old man in the dead of night. Great, Lúcia said. We have to take good care of the poor little fellow.

The old man improved somewhat. The milk agreed with him, and sometimes he accepted a grated apple, a small banana mashed up with sugar and cinnamon, some broth, some mashed potatoes. But he never rose from his mattress; he was always lying down, apathetic. And he never talked; we didn't know who he was, where he came from.

Looking after him was no picnic. He was unable to feed himself; he befouled the mattress. We had to change him twice a day; we washed his clothes at home, in secret, of course, then took them to another empty lot, a good distance away, to dry. A real hassle. Frankly, I was fed up with the whole thing. I couldn't wait to get out of this situation.

The old man noticed my ill will. Whenever I walked up to him, he started to cry; sometimes he tried to claw at me, or to bite me. Lúcia thought it funny: He doesn't like you, she would say.

He liked her. It was obvious. As soon as we entered the room, he would reach his fleshless, puny arms to her. Lúcia would cuddle him, kiss him, talk to him as if he were a baby; sometimes she would lay his head on her lap, and the old man would purr contentedly. Which would upset and annoy me. A dirty old man, that's what I thought he was. Or he wouldn't be rubbing himself against the girl like that. And that's what I said to Lúcia: He's a dirty old man. She took offense, and wouldn't talk to me. Later we made up, but only after I apologized not only to her but to the old ragamuffin as well.

One day we found him dead; apparently, he had suffered a heart attack, or something like that. Lúcia was inconsolable: Why now, when he was getting better? she kept saying in tears. I did my best to comfort her, then I saw to it that the old man was buried. Right there, in the empty lot. That night I got a spade from my house, then I dug a hole, into which I placed the body, wrapped in a blanket that used to belong to my grandfather. After covering him with earth, I put some stones and branches on top, and presto, the deed was done.

Many years later, a huge apartment building was erected on that empty lot. After we got married, Lúcia and I went to live there. We have two children, a boy and a girl. We're very unhappy. Sometimes Lúcia says that our unhappiness stems from the fact that we live atop the old man's bones. I don't think so. After all, the building stands twelve stories high, and we live in the penthouse. Many many meters above good and evil.

PROGNOSES

THE MILLIONAIRE TEOBALDO HAS HIS OWN PHYSICIAN. THE function of the physician is, first, to give Teobaldo a monthly checkup; second, to frighten him. To frighten him to death. Almost to death. The tests, the physician says gloomily after one such checkup, have revealed cancer. "Oh no," says, Teobaldo, turning pale (a genuine, not a put-on pallor). "And is it serious, doctor?"

"Deadly," says the doctor, dryly.

"How much time do I have left? Two, three years?"

"Less than that."

"Five, six months?"

"Afraid not."

"Weeks, then?"

"Should you be so lucky."

"Will there be pain?"

"Excruciating. Nothing will allay it."

Teobaldo bursts into tears. He weeps convulsively until suddenly:

"It was a lie!" the doctor cries out.

Teobaldo raises his head, his eye still brimming with tears, but he's already smiling.

"A lie, Doctor? Was it all a lie?"

"A lie, yes. A lie."

"It wasn't cancer?"

"No."

"Not even a benign tumor?"

"No. You're in the pink of health." The physician extends his hands. "Come on, let's shake on it."

Teobaldo clasps the doctor's hand, and then, he leaves, light-hearted. About two weeks later he is back, and the doctor says: "Your blood pressure is way up, your kidneys are not functioning well. I foresee a stroke in the near future."

"Is it serious, Doctor?"

"Terribly serious. Serious enough to send you to the intensive care unit."

"And my chances?"

"Slim. But even if you were to survive the stroke, paralysis will be inevitable, you'll never be able to speak again. . . . Reduced to a vegetable. A bedridden vegetable."

"But—"

No buts: Ruthless, the doctor continues to describe the picture: Spoon-fed like a baby. The cleansing of the private parts performed reluctantly by an orderly; a brute of an orderly, who very likely says humiliating words to his charges, and even hits them. Fits of crying for no reason. A burden to the family. Why is he taking so long to die will be the question most often asked by friends and colleagues at the club by fellow party members. The newspapers will have the obituary in readiness.

The millionaire weeps until:

"It was a lie!" says the doctor, smiling.

Then Teobaldo smiles happily. But a month later the doctor

again: "I'm concerned. The tests have revealed a serious blood disease. . . ."

And so it goes. Teobaldo suffers and suffers. There was a time when the suffering gave place to instantaneous euphoria, to an exceedingly heightened faith in reality, to an iron disposition to suffer the reverses of life, to an ever-increasing belief in the values of society. Lately, however, this hasn't been the case. Underlying the cathartic relief is a residue of disconsolation, of distrust, of bitterness. With bleary eyes Teobaldo studies the doctor's facial expression as he discourses on the degradation brought about by Alzheimer's disease: There's too much enthusiasm on the doctor's face. One of these days, the millionaire is thinking, it will be true. One of these days, I'll be lying on a hospital bed, weak, sick, worn down to a shadow. One of these days I'll have to change to a new doctor.

REAL ESTATE TRANSACTIONS

A REAL ESTATE AGENT MUST SELL A CONDO. IT'S A SUPERB APART-
ment: a four-hundred-square-meter penthouse in an eighteen-
story building, with four bedrooms, a living room with wide
floorboards, a terrace with a swimming pool and a sun deck. But
he can't find a buyer: the asking price is too high.

Then the real estate agent finds a potential buyer: a man,
young and rolling in money. This man is in a state of confusion.
He is going through a major crisis. He has walked out on his
wife. He wants to find out the meaning of all this. This what?
asks the real estate agent. This, replies the man, all this—life, the
world, everything. He has already searched for an answer in
books, he has already had several long conversations with a
priest, he has consulted a psychiatrist: in vain. In his despair he
has considered taking his own life by jumping out the window of
his twentieth-floor office. Not just to die; dying would be a side
effect of this fall—a by-product in which he is not particularly
interested; what he would like is to find the meaning of life in
the vertiginous trajectory leading to the asphalt.

The real estate agent is intrigued by what he has heard. Do you believe, sir, he asks, that you would then find the answer you've been searching for? Of course, says the man. But, persists the real estate agent, at what moment would you find it? At what distance from the ground? Ah, I wish I knew, replies the man. At one millimeter from the asphalt, perhaps? the real estate agent persists. The man smiles. Perhaps, except that it would be a bit too late, I'd rather have more time left—it would be nice if I could enjoy the answer for at least a few meters. This, reasons the real estate agent, would depend greatly on the speed of the fall; if the fall were to occur slowly, say, at the speed of a falling feather, you'd be able to find the answer sooner, let's say, at ten meters from the ground. After thinking for a while, the man agrees. The real estate agent then goes on: But suppose the fall were to be very, very slow, wouldn't it be possible for you to find the answer soon after jumping? I'd think so, says the man who, beginning to grasp what the real estate agent is getting at, is now all keyed up.

"And suppose that the fall were to be extremely slow, that the fall were to amount to practically motionlessness"—the real estate agent, triumphant, is now standing on his feet—"wouldn't it be possible for you to find the meaning of life at the exact moment that separates the intention to jump off from the act of jumping off?"

"Yes!" cries out the man, tears streaming down his face. "Yes, yes!"

Panting, the real estate agent sits down again.

"Then," he says slowly, "I have the solution for you."

Opening his briefcase, he takes out a photograph of the building and the blueprints.

"From the terrace of this penthouse here, you'll be able to find the meaning of life, should you wish to do so, sir."

The man writes out a check for a deposit: The deal is closed.

Days later the real estate agent is about to pay a visit to his client, now living in his new penthouse. He gets out of the car—and astonished, he stops short. In front of the building a crowd looking up: Way up, a man is standing on the edge of the terrace, ready to jump off. "Jump, jump!" many are shouting. "No, don't jump, don't!" shouts the real estate agent, overcome by anguish. Perhaps because the mob outshouts him, the man ends up by jumping off.

The real estate agent opens his briefcase: There it is, the receipt for the down payment that he was taking to his client. With a sigh he tears up the document. Then he gets into his car and speeds away, following a virtually horizontal trajectory.

LIFE AND DEATH OF A TERRORIST

FERNANDO WOKE UP STARTLED WITH THE ALARM CLOCK RINGING. He pressed the button down, sat up in bed, sighed. Sighing once more, he got out of bed and drew the curtains open. A beautiful day, he found out, and heaved yet another sigh: Beautiful days didn't agree with him. He'd rather have gray skies, which were more compatible with the emotional climate he needed to carry out his daily assignment. An assignment whose steps he reviewed as he shaved: 1) Pick up the small parcel lying on the kitchen table; 2) go to any neighborhood in the city, pick a store, a restaurant, or supermarket; 3) surreptitiously insert the parcel into a niche somewhere, or drop it into a garbage can; 4) affecting insouciance, leave the premises and go into a coffee shop across the street from the chosen commercial establishment; at the moment of the blast, run to the door and with the same expression of incredulous horror as all the other bystanders, watch the Dantesque scene of the bloodied bodies amid the smoldering rubble; 5) find a telephone, then dial a certain number; to the usual curt hello, say nothing but *perfect*. Mission accomplished. Chalk up another win.

He was sick and tired of the whole business. But there was no way he could get out of it. If only he had chosen some other occupation. If only he were, say, a bank teller in a quiet neighborhood bank: a peaceful, pleasant job. But no, he had opted for danger, for excitement. So, now he had to bear the consequences of his choice; and one of the toughest to bear was the transformation of what should have been a thrilling adventure into a tedious routine.

He got dressed, drank coffee, picked up the parcel. Before leaving, he cast one last look at the small apartment where he had been living alone since he separated from his wife. With a sigh he left. He got into his car in front of the building and started the engine. Before driving away, he hesitated: Where, today? The branch of a bank, it occurred to him, and he smiled at the thought. He headed for a distant neighborhood, then drove slowly along its tranquil streets until he arrived at a small bank. He parked and got out of the car.

He went in, greeted his fellow workers, and posted himself at the wicket. The security guard unlocked the front entrance and the first customers walked in. A lady came up to him, smiling. How are you, Dona Amélia? he asked. Fine, Senhor Fernando, you're always so nice. He took her check and handed her some money. And when she put it in her purse, he said: "Perfect."

Surprised, she looked at him.

"Perfect, what, Senhor Fernando?"

"Nothing," he said, smiling. "Everything. This day. Life. Everything, Dona Amélia. Everything's perfect."

"You have the soul of a poet," said Dona Amélia, touched. "You're like my late husband. He, too, all of a sudden would say beautiful things."

She said good-bye and left. Fernando attended to a few more clients, then chatted with the manager, and thus the morning went by. At lunchtime he took the parcel he had left under the counter and unwrapped it. A cheese and ham sandwich, at which he stared with a mixture of displeasure and satisfaction. I'm going to tear this thing to pieces in nothing flat, he muttered, and indeed, in six bites he devoured the whole sandwich. Perfect, he said, when he finished.

RESURRECTION

ONE OF THEM WAS TWELVE YEARS OLD; THE OTHER, THIRTEEN. They were sitting on the beach—deserted at that hour, five o'clock in the afternoon. All of a sudden:

"Look, there's a man over there," said the first boy.

"Where?" The second boy, who was tracing lines on the sand with his finger, raised his head and and looked, but without great interest.

"Over there. In front of the surf."

"I don't see anything."

"There, see. Over there. Can't you see his little head? Now it's gone. Look! Now it's there again."

"I don't see any head."

"Look carefully. Keep looking. It appears, then disappears. Look, there it is again."

"But how come I don't see anything?"

"Well, it's because ... Look, it has appeared again."

"I don't see anything."

"Look, there it is," persisted the first boy. "Follow the direction of my arm."

The other boy was already annoyed.

"I don't see anything. I don't think there's a man out there."

The first boy sighed.

"But there is. There's a man there. Now I can see his arm. He's waving his arm."

"I'll bet he's waving good-bye to you."

"Now he's gone again."

The other boy rose to his feet.

"Oh, shucks. I'll have to see this man. Even if it means going home and getting my binoculars."

The first boy was gazing at the sea steadily.

"Now he's gone. Gone, for sure. I don't see anything. No head, no arm, nothing."

"Just now, when I was getting the binoculars," says the other boy, skeptical. "Too much of a coincidence, isn't it? Quite a coincidence."

The first boy wasn't listening.

"He's gone, yes. Completely gone. Not a sign of him."

"Sure. As soon as I mentioned the binoculars—"

The first boy, who was younger, made no reply. In silence he sat gazing at the sea.

The second boy sat down again. He, too, was looking at the sea. In silence. Suddenly:

"Look over there," he said, pointing to the horizon. "Look, there's a man out there."

GENESIS

THE THREE OF THEM—FATHER, MOTHER, AND DAUGHTER—
were in a restaurant. The mother got up to go to the washroom. The girl, four years old, sat looking at her father, who was
chewing on his food in silence, a distant look in his eyes. Suddenly, she asked: "Daddy, how was I born?"

Perhaps because he was absentminded, he made no reply. She
asked again: "Daddy, how was I born?"

He looked at her but made no reply. He helped himself to
some more rice. She persisted.

"Daddy, how was I born?"

Putting down his fork and knife, he sat thinking for a few
moments. "You'd better eat and stop asking so many questions,"
he said.

"I don't want to eat. I want to know how I was born."

"Well." He took a sip of beer. "Do you really want to
know?"

"Yes."

"It was like this: First Daddy met Mummy, he liked her, and they got married. There was a beautiful wedding party."

"Was I there?"

"No. You weren't born yet. And that's what I was about to tell you: Daddy and Mummy got married. Then they wanted a little daughter. After a while Daddy began to feel a strange thing on his back. Mummy took a look and said: You have a little mole there."

"A what?"

"A little mole. A little lump. A very tiny lump. Daddy ignored it; but the tiny lump started to grow, so he went to the doctor."

"My doctor?"

"No. Another doctor. He said it was nothing, and told me to rub on it some of the ointment that he prescribed."

"Like the one Mummy rubs on me?"

"Yes. Except that in Daddy's case, it didn't work: The lump kept growing until it became the size of a ball."

"As big as my ball?"

"Bigger. By then Daddy was quite scared. He went back to the doctor, who ordered an X ray."

"What's that?"

"It's a kind of picture that shows what's inside people. But let me finish the story, will you? As I was saying, they took the X ray and the doctor said: Hmm, there's a tiny creature in there, it's small but it's going to get bigger."

"And did it get bigger?"

"It did. The swelling got so big that Daddy could hardly walk. He had to lie on his side. And he grew thinner and thinner. The bigger the swelling grew, the smaller Daddy grew. It looked as if Daddy was going to disappear."

"And did you disappear?"

"No. Don't you see I'm right here? I didn't disappear. One

night that huge swelling burst open, and a little girl sprung out. It was you. That's how you were born."

"Ah," murmured the girl.

The mother was back from the washroom.

"What have the two of you been chatting about?" she asked, smiling.

"I was telling our daughter here," he replied, "that we found her inside a head of lettuce. Isn't that right, daughter?"

"Yes," she said. Lowering her head over her plate, she began to eat.

*Available in a Ballantine Mass Market Edition.